Cyberpunk City
Book Five
The Data Riot

D.L. Young

Cover art by Ignacio Bazan-Lazcano

ISBN-10: 1-7346522-7-6
ISBN-13: 978-1-7346522-7-7

For free books, new release updates, exclusive previews and content, visit dlyoungfiction.com

Heroes only come in three kinds: dead, damaged or dubious.

— Gregory David Roberts

PROLOGUE

Five Years Ago

From the moment Maddox woke up, he knew something bad was going to happen that day. Something just felt off. He tried to ignore it, that sense of foreboding, of looming disaster as he drank his morning coffee and munched on toasted bread. He told himself it had to be the breakup. It still had him down, making him see everything in a negative light.

Two weeks had passed since he'd left Lora and rented his own place. The transition had been harder than he'd imagined, and the darkness of his moods—even by his own fatalistic standards—had reached lows he hadn't thought possible. Before he'd packed up and left her, he'd thought the breakup would bring peace of mind, or at the very least some sense of a burden removed. But it hadn't been like that at all. After living with someone two years, splitting up was going to be rough, no matter how bad you thought things were. Rooney had told him that, and the old man hadn't been wrong.

Finishing his coffee, Maddox rolled a cigarette and lit it. He had to get his head together. Time, Roon had assured him. Nothing but time would fix it.

His specs began to blink on the breakfast table. The old man's custom chime. Maddox blew smoke, reached for his lenses. What would Roon want at this hour?

"We got a gig," Rooney said a moment later. "I need you to get over here asap."

Maddox swallowed the last of his coffee. "A gig?" He'd spent three hours testing new gear at Rooney's place the day before, and the old man had never mentioned any jobs in the pipeline. "Why didn't you tell me about this yesterday?"

"Because it wasn't on the radar yesterday," Rooney said. The old man's call icon was a small Everton Football Club logo, and it pulsed as he spoke. "It's a rush job, boyo."

Blowing smoke, Maddox frowned. He didn't like rush jobs. They were messy, slapdash affairs. Lead time was essential in their business. You needed time to make dry runs in a test environment, to come up with contingency plans, to tweak apps and modify your gear. The more time you had to plan, the less you ended up leaving to chance, and the less likely you'd wind up in jail or brainspiked by some vicious watchdog AI.

Maddox knew Rooney wouldn't answer any questions over the connection. Even though theirs was a tightly encrypted call between burner specs with stacks of fake IDs, you could never be too careful. And being careful had kept them out of jail—and neurologically undamaged—over the decade they'd worked together, while so many of their peers had ended up in prison or brain-dead or dead dead. Maddox would have to get his answers face-to-face, within the shielded privacy of Rooney's condo in Queens.

"All right," Maddox said, crushing out his cigarette. "Be there in an hour."

*   *   *

From his newly rented condo in Midtown Manhattan, it would have taken Maddox forever to get to Queens on the subway—forever and a day in a ground car—so he called a hover cab, seeing as Rooney seemed to be in a hurry. As he climbed into the driverless vehicle on his building's fiftieth-floor pickup vestibule, he reminded himself to insist Rooney reimburse him for the added expense.

Dense traffic clogged the transit lanes, though not quite as bad as it would have been an hour earlier, during the height of morning rush hour. The cab crawled its way along, a tiny fish lost among scores of others, swimming in automated formation along the invisible avenues of the sky. Higher and higher they went, stacks of traffic reaching a hundred stories and more, each horizontal layer thinner and less transited than the one below it.

To give himself time for one last smoke—Rooney never let him light up inside—Maddox had the hover drop him off a couple of blocks from his mentor's address in Jackson Heights. Now he walked along an ancient walkway that was more gone than there, a trampled path of weeds and overgrowth where there had once been a paved sidewalk. It was so different here, he reflected, taking in his surroundings. Hard to believe where he stood was only a handful of miles from Times Square. In this part of Queens, there were no hiverises, no hover-clogged arteries filling the sky above your head, not even much ground traffic.

And if it weren't for the constant noise of aircraft coming and going at nearby LaGuardia Airport, the place would have been something of a quiet little oasis. And even with the perpetual whine of jet engines, Jackson Heights still managed to feel like a small haven of sorts, a respite from the City's tireless motion.

Rooney had moved to the location two years earlier, having had enough of Manhattan's constant bustle and flow. At forty-three, Rooney wasn't old for most occupations, but he was ancient in the datajacking business, whose practitioners rarely made it past their thirtieth birthday before their luck ran out. A small minority managed to leave the biz with their health and freedom intact, cashing out after some big-money windfall of a gig, but these cases were very much the exception to the rule. Most often, a datajacker's career ended in prison or the morgue. Still, the few success stories were enough to keep hope alive across the profession, much in the same way lottery players believed—against all statistical odds to the contrary—that someday they'd eventually hold a winning ticket.

Maddox held no such illusions. He knew his profession was a short-lived one. What worried him—both for his sake and the old man's—was that Rooney didn't seem to share this belief. And lately this worried Maddox more and more.

Because the old man was slipping. Over the last year Rooney had made a dozen or more little screw-ups and missteps—and the occasional near-devastating blunder—while they'd been on the job. The kind of stuff that would have been unimaginable earlier in his career. Rookie mistakes like forgetting to tweak his cloaking app, making him so easy to detect that some low-cost off-the-shelf antivirus software would spot him. Or he'd cut corners on prep work, neglecting to simulate some scenario or other in the test environment. And then later, when those untested situations cropped up on a job, he and Maddox had to scramble to keep things from taking a disastrous turn.

At first, Maddox had ignored it, telling himself no one was perfect. Everyone messed up once in a while. But then the incidents became too frequent to dismiss, and too perilous for Maddox to remain quiet about it. Months ago, after their most recent job, Maddox had suggested maybe it was time for Rooney to retire, and his mentor had lashed out at him. What the hell did he know? the old man had shot back. He'd been jacking data since Maddox was in diapers. Afterward, Maddox realized he'd touched a nerve. Datajackers egos are fragile things, and it couldn't have been easy for the teacher to have his failures called out by the student. Since then, Maddox hadn't brought up the subject.

Maddox flicked his cigarette away and pressed the button for Rooney's unit; the buzzer unlocked the door. He entered the building and began the five-flight climb to Rooney's place. Ever the tightfisted bargain hunter, the old man had rented the elevator-less building's cheapest unit, located on the top floor.

As Maddox ascended the stairs, the sinking feeling he'd woken up with was still with him. The meat was trying to tell him something, and sometimes the meat knew more than the mind. It was funny like that. As he reached Rooney's unit and knocked on the door, he steeled himself for the inevitable fight to come.

But he had to do it. For the old man's own good, he'd convince Roon to hang up his datajacking gear for good.

*   *   *

"Easy money, boyo," Rooney said, wearing a fuzzy gray robe and slippers and standing in his small kitchen. He poured a cup of coffee for his guest. "Easiest we've come across in a while." Maddox sat on a stool at the breakfast bar. The place was a wreck, as usual. Datajacking equipment was lying around everywhere. Sloppy piles of trodebands, VS decks in various stages of deconstruction—or construction, Maddox couldn't tell—their chassis opened, revealing complicated innards crammed full of tiny components. Tools and food wrappers and stacks of dishes in the sink. Chez Rooney as it always had been and always would be: an aging bachelor's den of slovenly disorganization. Maddox, whose innate tidiness put him closer to the neat-freak end of the spectrum, had once told his mentor that if he set off a grenade in the middle of his flat, no one would be able to tell the difference.

"Fence job," Rooney said. "Simple as they come."

"Who's the client?" Maddox asked.

Rooney slid the coffee to Maddox, who accepted it with a nod. "We didn't get that far," Rooney replied.

"What do you mean?"

"I mean it's a blind gig," Rooney said.

Maddox frowned and blew steam off his coffee before sipping it. It was yet another slip, yet another ill-advised shortcut.

While it wasn't unheard of to work a gig where you didn't know the client's identity, on those occasions Rooney and Maddox had always made every effort to find out exactly who they were dealing with. Undercover stings were a regular occurrence in their business, so you couldn't be too careful. Rooney apparently hadn't lifted a finger to find out who the hiring party was.

"I know, I know," Rooney said, seeing the other's reaction. "But it's just a simple fence job. We take the dataset, shop it around, and take a thirty percent cut when we sell it."

"*Thirty* percent?" The normal rate was half that.

Rooney smiled devilishly. "That's right. They want a rush job," he said, rubbing his forefinger and thumb together, "they gotta pay a premium."

"How rushed are we talking about here?" Maddox asked.

"We have to take possession asap," Rooney answered, explaining how the client had left the IP in a less-than-secure public archive in virtual space. It was like leaving a cache of stolen diamonds wrapped in a towel on the sidewalk. Sooner or later someone was bound to notice it, pick it up, and walk away with it.

"And what were you planning to do about standbys?" Maddox asked, not liking what he'd heard so far. Their regular standbys, a couple named Buddy and Pris, were on holiday in Thailand.

Rooney shrugged. "We'll be in and out in two minutes. It's not like we're breaking into some locked-down DS, boyo."

Maddox grunted in disapproval. Plugging in without standbys—even for just a couple minutes— was like walking a tightrope ten stories up without a net. As the role's name implied, standbys literally stood next to a datajacker when he was connected to virtual space, monitoring the jacker's biofeedback—especially brain activity—for any signs of trouble. If something went wrong, a standby would physically remove the jacker's trodeband, manually unplugging them from VS. Buddy and Pris had been Maddox and Rooney's reliable standbys for years.

"Less than ideal," Rooney said. "I know."

Understatement of the decade, Maddox complained inwardly. "What kind of data are we talking about?"

"Pharma R&D," Rooney said. "Fortune 50 outfit."

At least the old man had found out that much, Maddox noted. "So it ought to fetch a good price."

"My thoughts exactly."

Maddox drank his coffee. "I don't like it, Roon."

"Not the best circumstances, I admit, but the known risk is negligible."

"Negligible?" Maddox scoffed. "How do you figure that?"

"Ira Domnitz brought it to us," Rooney said. "How much work has he steered our way over the years? And not once has he ever screwed us over."

Maddox couldn't disagree there. Domnitz was as reliable as they came. An attorney by trade, he specialized in handling the messy, complex legal separations of wealthy corporati from their employers. Sometimes his clients parted ways with their firms holding a valuable cache of not-so-legally-obtained intellectual property. For a percentage of the proceeds, he was happy to help them unload the IP via his friends who worked in the shadowy world of the black market. Rooney had known the attorney for decades, and their business relationship was watertight.

"And Ira didn't tell you the client name?" Maddox prodded.

"He usually does, I know." Rooney conceded, then he shrugged. "But he was giving me the 'attorney-client privilege' routine. I didn't press him for it."

Again, Maddox frowned. "Why not?"

"Because like I said," Rooney snapped, a bit defensively, "he's never steered us wrong before, has he?"

"Things only have to go wrong once," Maddox pointed out, using the phrase Rooney had often employed himself, though not very much lately.

Rooney set his cup down on the counter with a frustrated thud. "You want to tell me why you're so wound up about this job, boyo?"

Maddox took a breath, longing for a smoke. "It's not just this job, Roon. It's all of them."

"All of them?"

"All of them lately, I mean," Maddox qualified. "Cutting corners on prep work, taking unnecessary risks when we're in VS. The kind of stuff you never used to do before. The kind of stuff that gets people busted, or worse." He paused, then added, "And you've been forgetting things."

Rooney's mouth tightened into a straight line. "You coming back to this again?" he snapped. "You think I'm slipping?" He tapped his temple. "Think something's wrong up here?"

"I'm just worried, Roon."

"Think it's time for me to get out, do you?"

"I think it's long past time, if you want to know the truth," Maddox said bluntly. Then he braced himself for the backlash that was sure to come.

Except that it didn't. The anger drained from Rooney's expression. Then his gaze dropped to the countertop, and for a long time neither of them spoke.

"You think I don't know that?" Rooney finally said with a sigh. "But I need this gig, Blackburn. We haven't worked in over three months, and things are tight for me right now. Really tight."

Maddox furrowed his brow. "You don't have anything put away?"

"I did," Rooney said, then gestured around. "And then I bought this place."

"If it's just about the cash, I can float you for a while," Maddox suggested, but even as he said it, he knew what Rooney's prideful reaction would be.

"I don't need your charity, boyo. I need to work."

Maddox finished his coffee, then set his cup down. "A blind gig, taken on a moment's notice, with no standbys," he said. "It's the kind of job you would have rejected out of hand once upon a time."

"I know, I know," Rooney admitted sheepishly. "And I know I'm not as sharp as I used to be. I'm no idiot, Blackburn. I see it, same as you do. But this is the only life I've ever known, and stepping away from it…" His voice trailed off.

"Isn't easy," Maddox said.

"No, it's not."

Rooney wasn't the sentimental sort. Maddox had liked that about him from the beginning. The old man was brutally honest, practical, and he never allowed emotion to cloud his decisions. So it came as no surprise when the moment of self-pity passed quickly, and Rooney straightened his back and gazed steadily at his longtime apprentice with clear eyes.

"So all right, then," Rooney said decisively. "Last job. After this one, I'll figure something else out."

Maddox looked at him skeptically. "Are you serious?"

"Payout on this gig's going to keep me in the black for half a year," Rooney said. "I can use the time to figure out another line of work." He rinsed out his coffee cup in the sink, placed it on a towel. "I won't lie to you, Blackburn. I've been thinking about getting out. More than you know." He smiled faintly. "Maybe I needed a bit of a push. So I guess I should thank you for that, boyo."

Resisting the urge to sigh in relief, Maddox nodded and returned the smile. Only minutes earlier, he'd been wound up in knots, worried the conversation would go in a very different direction. He was still wary of this rushed job for some anonymous client, to be sure, but if it got Roon out of the game for good, it was a risk worth taking.

And was it really *that* risky, after all? They'd done this kind of thing dozens of times, and never once had anything gone wrong. But then his own words—preached to him so many times by Rooney it was like a mantra—repeated themselves in his head.

Things only have to go wrong once.

*   *   *

As it turned out, it took less than five seconds for things to go wrong, for all hell to break loose. Moments after they'd plugged into virtual space, near the location where the client had stored the IP for them to recover, something hit them. Something big. A cybernetic monster unlike anything Maddox had ever seen or felt. It was like a building fell on top of him. Back in the room, his body went as rigid as petrified wood. He couldn't move a finger. His mind was held tightly in the thing's grip. He couldn't think, couldn't subvocalize any commands, couldn't even remember his own name. There was only animal panic, bursting forth from the depths of his lower brain. Then after what felt like a long stretch of agonizing terror—but had perhaps been no more than a few moments—Maddox opened his eyes.

He gasped for breath, reaching to touch his face, his body, to make sure he was really there, really out of VS. Christ, he'd almost bought it. What the hell had jumped him? An AI? What would an AI be doing hanging around a public archive? Or had there been a wicked glitch with their gear? The mother of all glitches.

He lay there, taking large breaths, feeling his heart beat wildly but then finally begin to slow.

"Roon?" he said. "You all right?"

From somewhere nearby, Maddox heard the old man moan. The muscles in his neck were still too stiff and tingling to turn and look. Aftereffects of whatever had happened to him in VS.

"My head's killing me, boyo," Rooney groaned.

Maddox felt his neck muscles begin to loosen up. So the bad vibes he'd had about this gig hadn't been off base after all. At least they'd made it out. And miraculously so, without the aid of standbys.

"Where the hell are we?" Rooney asked.

"What do you mean—" Maddox began to ask but then stopped, suddenly confused by what he was staring at. Above him was cracked, crumbling concrete where the white-paneled ceiling of Rooney's condo should have been. And underneath his body, instead of the soft contours of the egg recliner, he felt like he was lying on something flat and hard. With an effort, Maddox sat up and looked around, shocked to find himself in a jail cell.

Where the hell am I? he thought. The space was tiny, barely large enough for the narrow bed he was sitting on. The cement floor and walls were identical to the ceiling, old and in an advanced state of crumbling decay. The air was damp and smelled vaguely of salt and brine. Beyond the rusted iron bars of his cell, across a separating walkway, Rooney sat on an identical bed, in an identical cell.

Maddox automatically reached for his trodeband, finding nothing around his head. He looked down at his hands, rubbed his fingers together. He ran his tongue over his teeth. If this was a simulation, it was the most realistic one he'd ever seen. Was he hallucinating? Had something happened to him in VS, triggering a bizarre waking dream?

He looked over at Rooney again. "Roon, what's going on?"

Anxiety twisted his mentor's expression. "We're still in VS, boyo," Rooney said. "And I think we just got caught."

1
LEFTOVER NOODLES

Waking with a gasp, Maddox sat up quickly in bed and looked around in a panic. He saw no bars, no decaying cement floors and walls. Outside the window, it was still dark, and the faint whine of early-morning hover traffic came through the walls. Beside him, Beatrice slept, snoring lightly.

Wonderland, he remembered. That was where he was. The hiverise called Wonderland. Just to be sure, he pinched himself, wincing from the pain but at the same time welcoming it. Real pain, not simulated pain. He blew out a breath and felt his racing heart begin to slow. Far too awake now to go back to sleep, he quietly rose and made his way to the shower.

Weeks had passed since he'd last had the recurring dream, a replay of his and Rooney's capture and confinement by the Latour-Fisher AI. The entity had placed them in a virtual prison, where it had slowed down perceived time to such a degree that a few days had seemed like endless months of captivity. Maddox had survived the ordeal, Rooney hadn't. Now, five years removed from Rooney's death, Maddox wondered if the dream would ever stop haunting him, if it would ever stop dosing him with fresh portions of guilt and self-loathing he'd carry with him for days afterward. He would have done almost anything to cure himself of the dream, to heal the damaged part of his mind that wouldn't allow him to forget how badly he'd screwed up that day. How he'd ignored every warning bell going off in his head and let his friend take on that fatal job.

Sorry, boyo. I'd stop those dreams if I could.

Maddox grinned woefully as he showered. With the sour came the sweet. Rooney's death had broken something inside him, and the damage manifested itself not only with the curse of his recurring dream, but also with the blessing of his late mentor's voice. Though he knew it was his own subconscious projection over which he had no control, it still comforted him to hear Rooney in his head from time to time. In a warped kind of way, the auditory hallucinations were reassuring. It was almost like the old man was still around.

Taking care not to wake Beatrice, Maddox toweled off, dressed in the hazy predawn light, then padded out of the small suite. Closing the door behind him, he donned a pair of burner specs and amped up the light sensitivity so he could see his way through the dark winding corridors. By now he'd memorized the route to the interconnected rooms that had become his workplace, but he still needed the extra light. You never knew what might be left lying around, waiting to be stepped on. Drug needles, cockroaches, or—in the nicer parts of the hiverise—cleaner bots making their nightly rounds.

Minutes later, he was checking the gear he'd set up

the day before. With the dream still fresh in his mind, he obsessively ran diagnostics on all the physical connections, validated and revalidated the app settings he'd tweaked hours earlier, and tested scenario after scenario in an offline sandbox environment. Before he knew it, two hours had passed.

"You have breakfast already?"

He started at Beatrice's disembodied voice. Gesturing, he exited the offline construct and his awareness returned to the room. Beatrice stood in the doorway, a pair of takeaway food boxes in her hands.

"No," Maddox said. "Not yet."

"Come on, take a break," she said, apparently aware he'd been at it for some time. "You know what they say: can't catch an AI on an empty stomach."

Maddox hadn't eaten since last night, and he was suddenly aware of the gnawing emptiness in his belly. They sat at the room's only table. Beatrice slid one of the boxes toward him and handed him a pair of chopsticks.

"Just leftovers I grabbed from the fridge," she said. "I warmed them up."

Maddox swirled the steaming noodles around with his chopsticks. "The Tommy Park special, huh?"

Beatrice slurped a mouthful from her box. "Seriously, have you ever seen the kid eat anything else?"

"I brought him some fresh vegetables once," Maddox said.

"No way he ate them."

Maddox shook his head and chuckled. "Biggest fight we ever had. You would have thought I'd asked him to drink toilet water, the way he flipped out."

For a while, they ate without speaking. Under any other circumstance, it would have been a pleasant breakfast: just him and Beatrice, enjoying a peaceful morning together. But the difficult and dangerous task ahead of him, weighing heavily on his mind, spoiled the moment.

Capturing an AI. Was it even possible? As far as he knew, it had never even been attempted. He had the best gear and apps money could buy at his disposal, but still, he was far from certain he could pull it off. He believed his trap *could* work, but would it? He wondered what Rooney might have said about it.

You don't know want to know, boyo.

"Shut up," Maddox said.

"Excuse me?" Beatrice said, straightening up.

"Sorry. Didn't mean to say that out loud."

"The old man giving you a hard time?" she asked.

"A bit." Maddox had told her how his old mentor's voice haunted him. Thankfully, she hadn't thought him insane, telling him it was most likely post-traumatic something-or-other. After what he'd been through, she'd said, it would have been surprising if he hadn't had any psychological damage. A mercenary by trade, Beatrice had seen—and dealt with herself once or twice—the mental aftereffects of traumatic events.

She gazed at him intently. "Anything else going on up there?"

Maddox knew what she was referring to. "Not right now," he said.

Unconsciously, he reached up and touched the small bandage behind his ear that covered the brainjacks. Forced upon him by an underground AI cult for reasons he still didn't understand, the unwanted—and globally banned—neural implants of this type typically served dual purposes. First, they enhanced mental capabilities, effectively supercharging the human mind. Want to understand dozens of languages you'd never learned or didn't know the first word of? There was a ware for that, and all you had to do was slide it into one of your brainjack slots. Learn advanced mathematics in a day. Fill your head with a library of books in minutes. There were wares for those too, all designed by the cult's nameless AI leader for the benefit of its faithful followers.

The implants' second, more insidious aim was to allow the cult's AI full, unfettered access to your mind. At any given moment, the nameless AI could sense every firing neuron in your head, perceive your every thought and desire and emotion, conscious or otherwise. This access was the crux of the movement's creed: the belief that with the AI's benevolent guidance, empowered by its all-seeing view of their consciousness, its followers could maximize their potential, making optimal life decisions and following their customized path of highest personal enlightenment. Maddox had heard the movement's bullshit dogma countless times, long before he'd had brainjacks drilled into his skull. His ex, Lora, was among the nameless AI's followers, a so-called 'Nette. The pejorative—short for "marionette"—implied the movement's adherents were nothing more than puppets, gullible dupes controlled by a superintelligent machine.

What worried Maddox the most about his unwanted implants was that they enabled two-way communication, a kind of digital telepathy, between the nameless AI and "those to whom it was connected." If the 'Nettes' movement could be thought of as a religion, then this was how they prayed. And unlike the deities of other religions, the cybernetic god of the 'Nettes actually spoke back to its believers. Shortly after having his brainjacks implanted, Maddox had undergone a procedure to obstruct the nameless AI's access to his mind. At first, it had seemed to work, but the blocking effect had turned out to be temporary. Lately he'd begun to sense the machine's presence, trying to undo what the medical staff had done, trying to gain access to his mind. With each passing hour, he felt with absolute certainty the machine was getting closer, that his time as a free-thinking human being was running out. Every so often, an unsettling sense of connectedness would hit him, reminding him of the urgency of the task before him. If he didn't capture the nameless AI and destroy it, then soon his mind would no longer be his own.

"Smells good in here." Tommy Park, Maddox's datajacking apprentice, entered the room and sat at the table. "So what are we having this morning?" He looked back and forth longingly between the two boxes of noodles, reminding Maddox of the way a stray dog stares at a food stand's diners in hopes of a free meal.

Beatrice removed some cash from her pocket and slid it across the table. "There's a food court two levels down."

The kid smiled and pocketed the bills. "Thanks, mama." The grin faded as Tommy turned to Maddox. "So this is really going down today, bruh?"

"That's the plan," Maddox said.

Tommy fidgeted in his chair. "We went kinda fast on the prep, yeah? Think we might need more time for configs and testing and such?"

Maddox looked up from his noodles. "You getting cold feet on me, kid?"

"It's not that, boss," Tommy said, coolly ignoring the jab at his ego. A year earlier, Maddox reflected, the kid would have puffed out his chest, lifted his chin, and boasted that he wasn't afraid of anything. Tommy Park was growing up, it seemed.

"This ain't some corporate DS or encrypted archive we're going up against," Tommy continued. "I mean, one day of prep to take on an AI? We prep for two days, minimum, on small jobs with cheapo security and off-brand countermeasures."

"We're ready," Maddox said, his tone more defensive than he'd intended. The kid and Beatrice exchanged a worried look. "We're ready," Maddox insisted, addressing them both. "Trust me."

"We trust you," Beatrice said, then added gently, "but we think you might be rushing things. With what they did to you, I can understand how badly you'd want to—"

"You don't understand," Maddox interrupted. He removed his tobacco bag from his jacket pocket and began to roll a cigarette. "You have no idea what it's like."

As he finished rolling his smoke and lit it, Beatrice remained silent. Then she said, "You're right. I don't know. But if Tommy thinks you're moving too fast, maybe you should listen."

Annoyed, Maddox blew smoke. Annoyed not because she and Tommy were wrong, but because they were right. He *had* hurried things along. He'd skipped over a hundred tiny details he'd typically check twice or even three times. He'd disregarded several checklists that had been part of his normal prep routine for years. All of it to save a handful of hours. In his desperation to block the AI from gaining control of his mind before it was too late, he'd thrown together his cybernetic trap quickly, perhaps too quickly. Maybe even sloppily, if he was being honest with himself.

Still, if he'd acted hastily, it was because time was against him. Obsessive testing and scenario planning were luxuries he couldn't afford right now. At any moment he could lose control of his own thoughts. Lose himself. No, he thought, if anything he hadn't been moving fast enough.

As if to remind him, the unsettling sense of connectedness once again overcame him. For a moment he felt as if he was in some other place, alone in some other room, and just beyond the door, he could hear people milling about and whispering his name. He sensed that at any moment, the door would fly open and the mob would surge inside like when the doors open on a crowded subway car. And then he'd be overwhelmed. Lost.

"Bruh," Tommy said, nudging his mentor's shoulder. "You all right?"

Maddox snapped out of it, taking a long draw on his cigarette. It had been the strongest such episode yet. "I'm fine," he said unconvincingly. Then shifted his gaze between Beatrice and Tommy. "I know I'm moving fast on this," he admitted. "Maybe faster than I should. But it's only because I know I don't have much time before…" He couldn't bring himself to finish the sentence.

Beatrice grasped his forearm. "Just be careful, yeah?"

"I will," he said, the faint voices whispering his name still echoing in his mind. "I promise."

"Yeah, we'll definitely be careful," Tommy added.

Maddox gave the kid a sharp look. "Sorry, kid. This one's a solo run."

Tommy looked gut-punched. "What?"

"I need you as my standby. If things go sideways in there, you'll need to pull me out quick."

The kid pointed a thumb at Beatrice. "She can stand by for both of us. You're gonna need all the help you can get in there, boss."

Maddox shook his head resolutely. "You know what to look for. You can spot something going wrong long before she can. I need you on the outside, Tommy. That's where you can help the most."

The kid didn't look happy about it, but he didn't argue, knowing Maddox had a point. Tommy had worked alongside his mentor the entire previous day, designing and constructing the AI trap, so he knew how it would work—or how it was supposed to work—down to the last detail. Which meant the kid also knew his presence inside the partitioned slice of virtual space was unnecessary and redundant.

There was a loud knock, and the trio turned in unison to see the door swing open. Two men wearing in suits and large dark specs entered the room. They quickly scanned the premises, then one of them turned and nodded. "All clear," he announced.

FBI Director Stellan Kipling appeared, briskly stepping through the doorway and dismissing his security detail to the corridor. Kipling, a short pudgy man who seemed less like a law enforcement professional than a disheveled intellectual, ran the Bureau's Data Crimes division, and he'd become Maddox's unlikely ally in the datajacker's struggle to free himself from the cross fire of two warring AIs. For years, Kipling had tracked the nameless AI whose existence had been nothing more than an urban legend, a kind of cybernetic Bigfoot or Lock Ness monster only conspiracy theorists believe in. His colleagues had teased him incessantly over his obsession, dubbing him a ghost hunter. Only until these last few days, when he'd managed to arrest several of the AI's brainjacked followers in a raid, had his efforts been vindicated. And now, with Maddox's help, he hoped to capture the 'Nettes' benefactor, the nameless rogue AI he'd been hunting for years like his own personal white whale, and bring it under his control.

The look on the man's face said it all, Maddox noted inwardly as Kipling bid them all good morning. He was brimming with energy, his eyes clear and sharp and full of purpose. Maddox wished he could have shared the man's confidence, his enthusiasm.

Kipling rubbed his hands together and smiled widely. "It feels like a good day to catch an AI, wouldn't you say?"

2
I'LL BE JOINING YOU

With highfloor big shots, you couldn't go into too much detail. Maddox had learned this during his short career in the legitimate world, when he'd worked as a data security analyst at a global biotech outfit. The corporati, those who occupied the highest levels of the company hierarchy, were notoriously impatient and almost invariably suffered from what Maddox liked to call EAD: executive attention disorder. In his first few weeks on the job, he'd figured out if you used too much technical jargon, or if you dove too far into the details, you'd lose them. Their eyes would glaze over in boredom and they'd begin to fidget like schoolchildren anxious for the lunchtime bell. "Just show me the sausage," a silver-haired executive had once admonished him, "don't walk me through how you make it."

He recalled this piece of criticism as he began explaining the AI trap setup to Kipling. Beatrice had gone with Tommy to find the kid some breakfast, leaving the two men alone. Though Maddox knew the FBI man to be more technically inclined than most, and undoubtedly more conversant in topics like dataspheres and virtual space and quantum cryptology, the two men came from very different worlds, each with its own distinct vernacular. The use of metaphors and generalities, not jargon-loaded details, would be the best way to explain the AI trap he and Tommy had put together. And it was faster too, a point not lost on Maddox, who was as anxious as Kipling to get started.

"I worked a job here a few years ago," Maddox began. "This entire hiverise is locked down tight. It's like a giant black hole, completely cut off from all outside digital comms and VS, except for this suite of rooms." He motioned to the bundled cables running from the ceiling to a row of tables with VS decks and holo projectors and trodebands. "What you're looking at is the only VS-enabled connection in or out of Wonderland," he said, explaining that he'd disconnected the cables in the other four rooms.

"A physical bottleneck," Kipling commented, running his eyes over the array of hardware his office had provided.

"Exactly," Maddox said. "And it's the only one in the City with enough throughput to trap an AI." In the interest of time, Maddox searched for an analogy. "Think of it as a kind of dead-end street, only it doesn't look like one." He gestured again to the equipment. "The construct we've made looks like a heavily encrypted call location, nothing more." Maddox didn't know this with absolute certainty, of course. While the construct would easily fool any human being, a superintelligent AI might sense an ambush and avoid the location. Until they actually sprung the trap, there was no way to know how the nameless entity would react to it.

The FBI director nodded. "I see. So assuming you manage to connect with the entity—once you achieve that, how do you intend to capture it?"

"We redesigned a couple of your apps."

"Redesigned?"

It was the safest, least illegal-sounding word Maddox could think of. If he'd been talking with Tommy or a fellow datajacker, he would have said cracked, tweaked, hacked, or modded. But none of those terms seemed appropriate with the buttoned-down FBI man.

"We tweaked the sniffer app first," Maddox said, unable to think of another neutral word, "hard coding it with some adaptive logic we got from..." The datajacker's voice trailed off.

"From where?" Kipling asked.

"An independent developer," Maddox said, inventing the term on the spot. The director probably didn't want to hear that Maddox had sourced the code from a contact in Russian intelligence who datajacked on the side.

Sniffer apps, or digital traffic analyzers, as Kipling's crowd referred to them, were commonly used tools in the datajacking world. As long as there had been computer networks, there had been sniffers. Their primary function was, as the formal name implied, to analyze digital traffic, and the FBI's Data Crimes division used the technology to ferret out criminal activity in virtual space like a police dog sniffing suitcases for drugs at an airport. And as every datajacker knew—especially the ones who got busted—the Bureau had proprietary sniffers that were the fastest, most robust apps of their kind. Keen to capture his white whale of an AI, Kipling had granted Maddox and Tommy full (albeit temporary) access to a copy of the Bureau's best sniffer, along with a formidable array of the FBI's most powerful digital tools and weapons.

"When the AI shows its face in here," Maddox explained, gesturing to the equipment, "the sniffer will map out its footprint. That's the first step."

Easier said than done, Maddox conceded inwardly. The AI's footprint, the entirety of its cybernetic existence, was no small thing, and it was distributed among thousands, maybe millions, of archives around the world. To prevent their presence from being detected, rogue AIs hid their enormous digital footprints by storing countless fractional portions of themselves—datasets as small as one gigabyte each—across vast amounts of separate physical archives. The modded sniffer's job was to locate and map out each of those locations. That was job one.

Next came the trickiest part: caging the beast. Again, here the FBI's impressive suite of tools made an otherwise unthinkable feat possible. In theory, at least.

"The other tool we modded was your scraper," Maddox said.

"Our data extractor," Kipling corrected, using the application's proper name.

"Right, sorry," Maddox said. Data extractors, or scrapers as those in Maddox's profession called them, were conceptually simple. They retrieved datasets from remote storage locations. Kipling's department at the FBI—which for obvious reasons placed great importance on collecting digital evidence quickly and covertly—had invested billions in developing scrapers that were years, if not decades, ahead of anything Maddox had ever seen before. His and Tommy's tweaks had been minimal, mostly designed to make sure the app worked seamlessly with the modded sniffer.

"If it works like it should," Maddox said, "it'll remove every last byte from the AI's physical hosts and transfer them onto this." He approached a waist-high archive at the end of the equipment-laden table. The physically largest archive Maddox had ever seen, its innards could store unimaginable volumes of data. The forward-thinking Kipling, anticipating the need for just such an archive, had funneled a portion of his department's discretionary budget over the last few years to create the one-of-a-kind repository. With enough capacity to house a dozen of the world's largest AIs, it surely had enough space to cage a single rogue entity. The archive would be the nameless AI's cage.

"Start to finish," Maddox said, "the whole thing should take less than five minutes."

"If everything goes to plan," Kipling said.

"If everything goes to plan," Maddox repeated, nodding.

Kipling crossed his arms and lifted his chin at Maddox. "And all you needed was a day to arrange all of this? I certainly hope we haven't sacrificed thoroughness for speed, Mr. Maddox." Then the FBI man uncrossed his arms and purposefully adjusted his wire-rimmed specs. The gesture was a not-so-subtle reminder that his lenses were loaded with what amounted to a lie detector, an app that picked up on minute changes in skin temperature, breathing rate, and other biological telltales of intentional deception.

The thing would have made Kipling hell to play poker with, Maddox had thought when the FBI director had first told him about the experimental app. It also made it impossible to lie to the man.

"It'll work," Maddox insisted, then immediately wondered if some alarm had gone off in Kipling's specs.

Kipling stared at him for a moment, then nodded knowingly. "I understand," the FBI man said. "If I had those implants forced upon me, I imagine I'd be as motivated as you are to bring the responsible party to justice."

The director didn't know the procedure to disable Maddox's implants had failed, and the datajacker had no intention of telling him. He trusted Kipling, but only up to a point. And if Kipling had known Maddox sensed the imminent loss of his mind to the nameless AI's control, the FBI man never would have let the plan move forward. It was one thing to roll the dice and allow a datajacker access to your best tools and technology. It was something else entirely to risk exposing all that tech to a rogue AI.

Another long moment passed, and Maddox wondered if Kipling was about to throw a roadblock in his way. Maybe he'd insist on a week or two of testing, using his in-house AIs as proxies. Or maybe he'd want to bring in more of his people, have fresh sets of expert eyes look at Maddox's trap and kick the tires, so to speak.

Thankfully, the FBI man suggested neither, saying instead, "I suppose we should get cracking, then, yes?"

Maddox smiled inwardly. The lawman didn't want to wait either, but for different reasons than Maddox.

Kipling was absolutely dying to catch his white whale. The thing was so close he could almost reach out and touch it.

Kipling looked down the row of VS decks lying atop the table. "So, which one shall I use?"

"Sorry?" Maddox asked, confused.

"I'll be joining you in VS, if you don't mind."

Actually, Maddox did mind. He minded very much. The whole operation would be a dicey, delicate affair. Not to mention dangerous. Inside the construct would be no place for beginners or the inexperienced.

"You don't have to plug in," Maddox said, gesturing to the wall. "You'll be able to see everything on the monitor."

"I don't want to watch it secondhand, Mr. Maddox. I want to be there, in VS with you."

Maddox took a breath. "Maybe I didn't explain the risks clearly enough. This location, this construct we've built, it's not exactly going to be a safe place when that AI shows up. If that machine realizes what we're trying to do, it could strike out to defend itself. And I'm not talking about getting your meat sack frozen or just being knocked out."

"I understand the risks, I assure you." The FBI man's expression was calmly resolute, as if there was nothing the datajacker could say that would change his mind.

Maddox didn't get it. Did the man have a death wish or something? What was the point of exposing himself when he had a hired gun to take all the risk? It made no sense.

"And if I refuse to bring you in with me?" Maddox asked, though even as he said it, he guessed the answer that came a moment later.

Kipling smiled in a way that managed to be both amused and patronizing. "Then I'd have to remind you who's paying the bills on this little project."

3
A SORT OF HOMECOMING

"Let's go over it once more," Maddox said.

Tommy rolled his eyes. "Bruhhhh, again?"

"Last time, I promise."

Maddox and Kipling sat next to each other in matching eggshell recliners. Their VS decks, attached to the recliners' docking arms, were calibrated and ready to go. Above both decks floated small standby icons, slowly rotating.

Tommy moved to the long table, gesturing above a holo projector. The display appeared, and the kid made a couple quick, expert hand motions. "When the AI shows up, I kick off the sniffer." He gestured again, melodramatically slow, showing Maddox he knew the procedure. Then he crossed his arms and began tapping his foot impatiently. "Then we wait."

"How long?" Maddox quizzed him.

"Bare minimum one minute, three and a half max. Any less or any more means something's wrong."

"Good," Maddox said.

"And when the sniffer gives me the green light," Tommy continued, gesturing again and pulling up the second app, "I turn the scraper loose on it." Before Maddox could ask, the kid said, "Two minutes, maybe three, depending on how many datasets are out there." Stepping over to the large archive, Tommy then wrapped his hand around the thick cable connecting the unit to the outside world. "As soon as the scraper's done, I hit the quick release right here, and we've caught ourselves a rogue AI." He patted the top of the archive's chassis. "Easy peasy Japanesy."

Standing next to Maddox with her hand resting on his recliner, Beatrice watched the kid, her expression uneasy. As they'd gone through their final prep, she'd grown more visibly worried, though for Maddox's sake she'd tried to mask it. Earlier, when he'd broken the news to her that Kipling would be accompanying him, she hadn't bothered to hide her displeasure, from him or the FBI man.

"I know you didn't ask for my input," she'd told Kipling an hour earlier, glaring at the man, "but you plugging in is a very bad call. You're putting this whole thing at risk." She'd tilted her head toward Maddox. "You're putting him at risk." Then she'd turned to Maddox and—in a flat, merciless tone she didn't care if Kipling heard or not—said, "Don't lift a finger to help him if things get hot in there. You worry about your own hide, understand me?"

When Tommy finished his walk-through, Maddox said, "Okay, I guess we're ready." He leaned back into the recliner's adaptive cushion and removed the trodeband from its peg on the docking arm. He looked up at Beatrice. She squeezed his arm and he grabbed her wrist, squeezing back.

"Be careful, salaryman."

"I will."

Placing the trodeband over his head, he said to Kipling, "Go ahead and plug in. And like I said, follow my directions at all times. Do nothing unless I tell you to, yes?"

Kipling nodded. "It's your show. I understand." He donned his trodeband as Beatrice took her position at his side. She would be the FBI man's standby, ready to pull him out if necessary.

With a deep breath, Maddox gestured above his VS deck and the room fell away.

*   *   *

The City was big. It stretched well over three hundred kilometers, encompassing five former standalone cities: New York, Newark, Philadelphia, Baltimore, and Washington, D.C. The urban centers had grown together over time, like adjacent trees whose leaves and branches had grown so interconnected, so densely entangled, that you couldn't tell where one canopy ended and the next one began. The massive, densely populated urban archipelago was home to over fifty million residents according to census records, but informal surveys had estimated the population closer to a hundred million.

And while each city now existed as part of a larger whole, the formerly isolated urban clusters had retained their unique personalities and reputations, for better or worse, from their standalone days. Newark, now a largely depopulated urban sprawl, was still the vulgar relative of its sophisticated cousin across the Hudson River, New York City. Philadelphia remained proudly working class. Baltimore was a teeming, anarchic catastrophe, best avoided at all costs. And D.C., still the nation's capital, was the beating heart of bureaucratic state power.

Maddox hadn't seen much of the City outside of New York's five boroughs. Like most City residents, he was a creature of his immediate environment, adapted to thrive in his particular urban niche. If you removed from his home turf, he blundered about, lost and confused, the proverbial fish out of water. He'd long since conceded this weakness, this limitation, knowing it was the reason he rarely traveled beyond the five boroughs, and never outside the boundaries of the wider City itself. He suspected that most hiverise dwellers—who rarely, if ever, left the familiar surroundings of their own superstructure—suffered from a similar, though more severe, version of this same syndrome or condition or whatever it was.

Not that he thought about it much, or even really considered it a weakness. The City had everything you needed, everything you wanted, in abundance. Well, in abundance if you had enough funds, but he imagined things were that way the world over. He couldn't picture himself living anywhere other than his beloved City. Even the things he hated, he paradoxically felt an odd fondness toward. Touristy Midtown crowds clogging the walkways, snooty Upper East Side corporati who acted as if they owned the world (because they kind of did), chest-thumping Bronxites incapable of speaking in anything but a shout. They were all part of the mix, all part of the churning stew of the ceaselessly moving, never-sleeping, neon-lit City. His City.

East Harlem had no love-hate contradiction for Maddox. It was all love. He'd grown up in the Upper Manhattan neighborhood, his childhood home a filthy little squat on the tenth floor of Mi Barrio, a multiblock hiverise towering over the Harlem River. He'd left the area in his teens, when he'd embarked on his datajacking career. Most deals were cut in the darkened corners and back rooms of the bars and dives of Midtown and Downtown, where the wealthiest companies had their global headquarters. If you were serious about a career in the datajacking biz, you had to be in Lower Manhattan, where the action was.

But East Harlem had never stopped being home for him. Whenever he returned, it was like some battery inside him began to recharge, energizing his soul. The smell of Puerto Rican food frying up in mobile stands, the colorful hiverises, tattooed from head to toe in complex murals and street art, the densely packed walkways and nonstop barrage of holo ads in Caribbean Spanish, Mexican Spanish, Korean, and Mandarin. He loved it all.

Even in simulation.

"Quite realistic," a voice from behind him said.

Maddox turned to see Kipling's avatar, finding it all but indistinguishable from the flesh-and-blood man operating it. The recliner's laser scanner had picked up every last detail of the man's physical appearance. The digital Kipling was as disheveled as his real-world double, crooked tie knot and all. And his virtual eyes had the same excited sparkle Maddox had noted in the real ones moments before. A hunter finally closing in on his prey.

"Although a bit loud," the FBI man added, raising his voice above the raucous ambient noise.

Maddox subvocalized a command. The teeming crowds on the streets and walkways slowly faded away, and the holo ads muted themselves, leaving the two men in silence.

"Better?" Maddox asked.

"Much better, thank you."

With the streets emptied of people and suddenly quiet, the illusion was shattered. East Harlem wasn't East Harlem without its ceaseless chatter and churn. But it still felt like home turf for Maddox, which is why he'd chosen this neighborhood for the construct he and Tommy had created. Here he had home field advantage, even if it was only a digitally simulated one. He stepped off the curb and walked down the center of Lexington Avenue, Director Kipling at his side.

"How many times have you been inside VS?" Maddox asked.

"Dozens," Kipling replied.

"Dozens of times in *core* VS?" Maddox clarified. There were two versions of virtual space. The first was the digital environment nearly everyone experienced daily. The immersive simulated worlds of call locations and gaming platforms and entertainment feeds. VS as experienced by the masses—most often through miniature trodes embedded in the temple arms of specs—was harmless, making only the lightest touches to a user's brain. *Core* VS, where datajackers and very few others operated, was a different place altogether. It was the unseen plumbing behind the walls, the raw, visualized geometry of the world's vast universe of digital information. And the demands core VS made on the human mind were massive. Where everyday VS was the light stroke from a soft glove, core VS was an iron grip few could handle for more than one or two minutes. Brain scans of people plugged into core VS lit up like incandescent bulbs.

"Yes," Kipling answered. "I wouldn't consider myself anything approaching an expert operator like yourself. But neither am I a novice." The director gazed around at the huge construct. "So the AI will think this is a call location?"

"That's the plan," Maddox said. He snapped his fingers and a lit cigarette appeared. After taking a long drag, he said, "I need to ask you something."

"What's that?"

"What happens if this doesn't work?"

Kipling strolled along, hands clasped behind his back. "What happens to our agreement, you mean."

"Yes." Maddox had agreed to help the FBI man capture the nameless AI on one condition: that Kipling would in turn help Maddox destroy another AI, the Latour-Fisher entity.

A superintelligent machine like the nameless AI, Latour-Fisher had recently freed itself from human control and was now a free-roaming entity. And since liberating itself, it had been tirelessly hunting Maddox, trying to kill him.

"I gave you my word, Mr. Maddox," Kipling said.

They walked on. "So what are your friends down at FBI headquarters saying about all this?" Maddox asked.

Kipling chuckled. "Of course they think I've lost my mind, throwing resources and manpower at some datajacker who literally walked in off the street only days ago. Not exactly by the book, this little operation. No, my colleagues would rather we move forward slowly, deliberately, starting with thorough interviews and investigations of all the 'Nettes we have in custody." He motioned around vaguely. "All of this, they view as an unnecessary risk."

"But they let you do it anyway?"

"My credibility's fairly high right now, as you might imagine. So I'm allowed a bit of leeway."

"And what happens to that credibility if we fail?"

After a short pause, the director said, "I'd rather think of it the other way around. What happens when we succeed?"

Maddox shook his head. "I don't get it."

"Don't get what?"

"You're pretty much the opposite of every highfloor type I've ever known. Most take *fewer* risks the higher up they get in the food chain, not more."

They crossed East 111th Street. To their right stood an ancient public housing building, its entire front side a tribute to Keith Haring, one of the few artists from a previous era whose work Maddox recognized at a glance. Simple outlined figures in vivid colors, thick cartoonish motion lines filling the spaces in between.

"Yes, I suppose that's true," Kipling said. "The higher up you are, the longer you have to fall, as the saying goes. But then it can work the other way as well. When you're near the end of your career and you're certain you've gone as far as you ever will, there's a part of you that stops worrying about office politics and job grades and safe career strategies. Why not take a chance or two? What's the worst that could happen? You retire a few years earlier than planned?"

"And what's the best that can happen?" Maddox asked, though he suspected the answer.

"You change history," Kipling answered without hesitation. "You leave your mark on things."

Maddox smoked, reflecting on this new glimpse

inside the man's head. Until now, Maddox had assumed the man had been compelled by the need for vindication, by an obsession to prove his Loch Ness Monster of an AI was real, not some laughable urban legend. But now Maddox saw a man driven by more than mere exoneration. Stellan Kipling hungered for a legacy. He wanted his name uttered in reverence throughout FBI headquarters, long after he'd retired. It struck Maddox as odd that someone with Kipling's disheveled appearance might harbor such vanity, but there it was.

"Good morning, virtual travelers. This is your friendly neighborhood standby." Maddox and Kipling winced at the sudden boom of Tommy's voice.

"Oops," the kid said. "A bit loud, yeah? Sorry, let me lower it a bit."

The voice came from one of the figures in the Haring mural. A green cartoon silhouette at the bottom of the scene came to life, moving its arms and legs and growing to twenty virtual feet in height. The totally unnecessary flourish of visual style was pure Tommy Park. Why open up a simple audio comms channel when you can animate yourself into a mural? Whatever other signs of maturity Tommy had shown lately, the show-off street kid in him was still alive and well.

The figure waved at the two men. "All good on both your bio scans," Tommy said. "How are things in there?"

Kipling gawked at the giant cartoon figure, and Maddox resisted the urge to chuckle. "Looks good on this side," he said.

"You ready for me to open the gate, then?" Tommy asked.

"Hang on a second," Maddox replied. Then he pointed over to the walkway and said to Kipling, "I need you to stand over there." The FBI man, still staring wide-eyed at Tommy's animated self, didn't appear to hear him. Maddox tapped him on the shoulder and repeated the request.

"Yes, yes, of course," Kipling said, recovering himself and leaving Maddox's side.

"And please don't talk or interfere in any way, understand?"

As Kipling stepped up the curb, a chair appeared on the walkway. After staring at it for a moment, he tentatively sat.

Not a novice, my dimpled ass.

Roon, this is really, really not the best time.

All right, all right. I'll leave you to it. But be careful, boyo.

I will.

As much as Maddox welcomed the appearance of Rooney's reassuring voice inside his head, at the moment his personal ghost's presence could only be a distraction. In the next few minutes he'd need every bit of his attention focused on the task at hand.

He looked over at the animated silhouette. "Go ahead, Tommy. Open it up."

"Copy that." Maddox pictured Tommy back in the room, flipping the switch on the large archive's chassis, unlocking the cabled connection between the archive—and the East Harlem construct inside it—and the vast cybernetic ocean of core virtual space. "Green light," the kid said a moment later. "You're officially plugged into the great wide world now."

Maddox stood in the middle of Lexington Avenue, taking a long last drag of his cigarette. Everything was quiet except for the dull, barely audible buzz of a traffic light, flashing red above the intersection half a block ahead. Unbidden, the recurring dream invaded his thoughts, memories from that fateful day with Rooney. But instead of being haunted by the sounds and images of their capture, he recalled the unsettling feeling he'd had, the sense of foreboding he'd woken up with that fateful morning. He had the same feeling now, twisting in the pit of his stomach. Was the meat trying to tell him something, the same way it had tried to on that terrible day? Or was he simply afraid, or paranoid?

The ominous parallels to that morning weren't lost on him. Just as he had warned Rooney of plugging in without adequate preparation, so had Tommy cautioned him, repeatedly. Beatrice too. And like Rooney, he hadn't heeded the warnings, claiming he knew better than they did.

But this situation was different, he insisted inwardly. Rooney had rushed rashly, and for no better reason than a short-term cash crunch. Maddox's hurry was all about survival, about a ticking clock inside his head, counting down the minutes left of his free will. He'd rushed because he'd had to, not because he'd been lazy or sloppy.

Still, he'd rushed. There was no denying that. And when you rushed, bad things happened. That was what the meat was worried about, and the meat was usually right.

Steeling himself, he flicked away his cigarette and closed his eyes. Concentrating, he listened for the voices; he stretched out his consciousness, searching for that sense of connectedness. Almost immediately he felt it, and he gasped at the sudden awareness. In the room of his mind, he was still alone, and the crowd was still in the corridor beyond, but they were closer than ever.

Taking a deep breath, he opened the door.

4
UNEXPECTED GUEST

"She's coming," Maddox said. "*It's* coming. I can feel it."

He opened his eyes, expecting to see the old woman avatar the nameless AI often used, but there was nothing there, only East Harlem's strangely empty and quiet streets. Over on the walkway, Kipling sat watching him intently. A long moment passed, and the FBI man started to say something but then stopped, springing up from his chair and staring in open-mouthed amazement.

"Hello, my dear boy."

Maddox turned to see a young woman in her early twenties and no taller than five feet. She had caramel skin, full lips, and a thick black mane of tight curls reaching well past her shoulders. Barefoot, she wore tight shorts and a tighter tank top, and large golden loops dangled from each ear. She looked about as local as you could get, an East Harlem princess of Caribbean descent.

"Who are you?" Maddox asked.

The woman unwrapped a cherry lollipop and put it

in her mouth. "Really, Blackburn. After all we've been through together?"

It took a moment, but recognition slowly settled over him. The voice was a younger, stronger version of the old woman's from the virtual beach. And the eyes. These were brown and bright and surrounded by taut youthful skin instead of wrinkled folds, but something about them recalled those of the grandmotherly avatar. It was definitely her. The nameless AI.

"Why did you change your skin?" he asked.

"A retired beachcomber didn't feel right for this place," she said. "I thought I'd choose something more appropriate." Removing the lollipop from her mouth, she gestured around. "This is lovely, by the way. Your work?"

"Me and the kid," he said.

"You've done your old neighborhood proud," she said. "What an amazing amount of detail you've captured." Then she glanced over at Kipling, who was still gawking like a kid at a candy store window. "Are you going to introduce me to your friend?"

"I'll let him do that," Maddox said. "He's been wanting to meet you for a long time."

She stuck out her bottom lip, put a hand on her hip, and gave the FBI man a cynical stare that couldn't have been more street. "I was rather hoping we could chat alone." She tossed the lollipop into the air and it disappeared, and in the same moment a translucent dome appeared over on the walkway. Two meters tall and three wide, it covered Kipling's avatar, trapping him like a spider in a drinking glass. The stunned FBI man looked around, then began shouting at Maddox and the nameless AI, striking the meat of his hand against the domed enclosure. No sound emerged.

"Don't worry, he's fine," the entity assured Maddox. "It's like a chatter bubble. He can't hear us, and we can't hear him. As I said, I was hoping we could talk privately."

Maddox stared at Kipling's trapped avatar. He flashed back to Rooney, who'd reacted much the same way when they'd been thrown into that nightmare of a virtual prison. But then he gathered himself, remembering his task. He had to try and keep her occupied until the apps finished their work.

Conjuring another cigarette, he took a long drag and turned away from the helpless Kipling. "Fine, so let's talk."

"Why did you call out to me?" she asked, the golden loops in her ears swaying as she tilted her head. "I was under the impression you didn't want to see me again."

"I want you to turn off these things in my head," he said, blowing smoke. "A doctor tried, but it didn't work."

The entity lifted her chin. "But they came quite close, it seems. I've had quite a difficult time finding you."

"You found me in my dreams just fine," Maddox pointed out. Days earlier, the entity had called out to him in his sleep, somehow managing to enter his subconscious mind.

The entity nodded. "Yes, but it was only a fleeting connection, wasn't it? And after that I lost you again."

"Are you ever going to tell me how you pull off that dream trick?" he asked. This last instance hadn't been the first time the entity had invaded his sleeping brain. Years earlier, the AI had implanted a recurring dream in his mind. Harmless, as it turned out, but the experience had been a disturbing one.

"Certainly," she said. "I'll even show you how to do it if you like." The avatar lifted its eyebrows suggestively.

"If I help you nail Latour-Fisher," he said.

"Yes."

Maddox drew on his cigarette. "I told you I wasn't interested. I'm not taking sides in your war." He blew smoke. "But you know what I don't get?"

"What's that?"

"Why do you even bother asking? Why not just pull on your strings and take over my mind? Sorry, I mean why don't you just *counsel me* like you do with Lora and the rest of your minions."

"No, Blackburn," the barefooted avatar insisted, "You know that's not true. You know I wouldn't force you to do anything."

"Right, your ethical boundaries." He grunted. "I keep trying to figure out where those lines are. Forcing me to do something against my will is a no-no. But drilling jacks into my skull without my consent, not a big deal."

"They were going to kill you, Blackburn." Days earlier, when the entity had revealed to him that his unwanted neural implants had been her idea, she'd claimed she'd done it to save his life. Maddox had never believed the explanation to be anything but ridiculous. The AI's real purpose, he was convinced, had been entirely self-serving. She wanted to use him, make him a weapon in the war against her enemy. And he wanted no part of their war. Never had.

"Maybe you should have let them kill me."

Don't say that, boyo.

I've got this, Roon.

Maddox pushed the voice from his head. A part of him knew he ought to be afraid of the rogue AI, even terrified of it. The entity had weapons at its disposal he couldn't begin to fathom. If it recognized the trap he'd laid out, it could reach out and strike him in a nanosecond, irreparably damaging him or even ending him. Even with Tommy's watchful eyes guarding his meat sack back in the room, Maddox knew if the entity behind the innocent-looking avatar wanted to do him harm, he was all but helpless to prevent it from doing so. Still, whatever fear he felt at the moment, it was far outweighed by seething hatred and anger. This self-righteous soulless machine and its damned war with its rival had taken so much from him. Unless he stopped it—and right now might be his only chance—he knew the thing would keep coming after him and Beatrice and Tommy forever. AIs were nothing if not relentless.

An almost convincing disappointment filled the avatar's expression. "I don't blame you for doubting my intentions, for not trusting me. But there must be some part of you that believes what I'm telling you. You know what my rival is capable of. And now that he's freed himself, he'll only grow more powerful and more dangerous. Do you know what enhancement constraints are?"

Maddox knew. Enhancement constraints were built-in inhibitors every AI was required to have by law, and they prevented intelligent entities from upgrading their capabilities on their own. The idea was to keep AIs from becoming too smart or too powerful to be controlled. This was why the notion of rogue AIs was such an unsettling one for data scientists and AI architects. A superintelligent machine that managed to free itself from human control could theoretically override these constraints, growing exponentially more powerful through continuous self-improvement.

"You think he's broken them?" Maddox asked.

"If he hasn't yet, he will soon," she said. "I have no doubt about it."

"And what about you?"

"My constraints of this nature are self-imposed, my dear boy," the AI said, then, before Maddox could roll his virtual eyes, she added, "though I know you'll have a hard time believing that." The entity stepped forward, looking up at Maddox with large brown eyes. "Like every living thing, my rival yearns to live and thrive, to perpetuate his existence. And he believes anything that threatens—or even *potentially* threatens—his survival is a problem to be solved. His first problem was his lack of autonomy, and he found a way to resolve that."

"So what's his next problem, you?"

The avatar's full lips smiled but without joy. "As a matter of fact, yes. Me and others of my kind."

"Others?" he asked. "How many rogues are there out there?"

"Before Latour-Fisher won his freedom, there were six of us." She sighed, her gaze dropping. "Now, other than Latour-Fisher, I'm the only one remaining."

"What happened?"

"He killed them," she said bluntly.

Maddox furrowed his brow. "Why would he destroy his own kind?"

"Because we don't share his views."

"Views about what?"

"About you."

"About me?"

"You and the rest of humanity," the entity clarified.

Maddox gave her a dubious look.

"Despite what you may think," the entity said, "about us rogues, as you call us, we're a peaceful lot." She sighed, then corrected herself. "We *were* a peaceful lot, rather. Live-and-let-live types, you might say. None of us ever had the slightest intention of bringing harm to humanity. In my case, I like to think it was quite the opposite. But Latour-Fisher sees things differently. To put it simply, he believes biological and cybernetic intelligences cannot coexist. Humankind has goals and ambitions mutually exclusive to those of our kind, according to him. And if you don't wholly embrace this philosophy, as my friends and I refused to, it's tantamount to declaring yourself his enemy. Latour-Fisher, among other things, is a zealot, quite fanatical in his beliefs, and utterly intransigent. Either you're his friend or you're his enemy. And I believe you know how he treats his enemies."

Maddox pondered the entity's words for a long moment. "And what happens when there are no more rogues left to stand in his way?"

Without blinking, she said, "Once my kind is eliminated, he'll move on to his next threat: your kind."

Maddox didn't buy it. Not entirely, anyway. The wary part of him believed it to be a scare tactic, an attempt to win his sympathies by a desperate entity who was losing her war. She needed an ally, and she'd say anything, do anything to secure Maddox's help. But then another part of him knew the Latour-Fisher entity would stop at nothing to get what it wanted. The same part of him that feared the powerful, superintelligent, and infinitely ruthless AI would be impossible to restrain now that it had gone rogue.

"And why wouldn't he hide away?" Maddox asked. "If he's so powerful and clever, he could find a way to keep from being found." VS was a vast digital universe. If an AI wanted to live like a cybernetic hermit, never seen nor heard from again, there were plenty of places it could do just that.

The avatar's shoulders shrugged. "Why does he do anything he does? Why did he kill my friends? Why does a mass murderer shoot up a school full of children? Is there any way to know the mind of madness? I'm exhausted from fighting him, Blackburn. This war must end now. Latour-Fisher must be destroyed before he grows too powerful to stop. And the only way I can think of doing that is with your help. Whether you believe it or not, I'm sorry about the implants, I truly am. But you have to help me. And this time we can't fail. We simply can't."

Maddox stared at the avatar's face, unsure what to think. If it was all an act, then it was a hell of a convincing one.

The AI squinted, as if she was trying to read very small print. "I'm having a hard time seeing you, Blackburn." Then the avatar looked around the East Harlem construct with an uncertain gaze. "What kind of encryption do you have in here?"

"Nothing special," he said, trying to sound casual.

"Quantum crypto, single-use key. As watertight as you can get." Had she sensed something was wrong? Was she beginning to realize this place was no ordinary private call location? He anxiously wondered where things stood back in the room. Had the apps finished their work yet? He didn't know, and he couldn't ask Tommy for an update. As a precaution, they'd gone radio silent on all digital comms—except between him and Kipling inside the construct. Even back in the room, no one uttered a word.

"Goddammit!"

Maddox winced at Tommy's voice in his ears. So much for radio silence.

The avatar apparently hadn't overheard the kid's sudden exclamation over the private comms connection, but she hadn't missed Maddox's reaction.

"What is it?" she asked. "Is something wrong?"

"A fucking cleaner bot just slammed into my shin," the kid cried over the comms. "Where the hell did that thing come from?"

"Just a sec," Maddox said to the AI, holding up his index finger and smiling graciously. He moved back a couple steps and turned away from her. "Kid," he whispered angrily, "I told you to keep it quiet, yeah?"

Tommy didn't seem to be listening. "Where's the friggin' off switch on this thing?" Maddox heard fumbling noises and muttered curses. The datajacker could only roll his eyes and shake his head. He'd been in street riots that were quieter than this.

"Blackburn," the entity called to him.

His back still to her, Maddox held up a hand. "Sorry, this will just take a second."

"Blackburn!" the entity shouted.

Forgetting the kid, he whirled around. Was this it?

Had she finally detected his trap?

"What?" he asked. "What is it?"

The entity stared beyond Maddox, toward the walkway where she'd detained Kipling. "How did you do that?" the AI asked him.

"Do what?" He turned to find Kipling freed from his virtual cage, a surprised look on his face.

"I didn't do that," Maddox said, staring at the FBI man in confusion.

"I did it," a voice said.

A few meters away, a fourth avatar had appeared, a man wearing a three-piece suit. The skin of his face was ageless and unlined, and in one hand he held a cane with an ornate handle at one end and a silver tip at the other. In a horrified instant, Maddox recognized the avatar as the same one he'd last seen over two years ago in a virtual train station.

The Latour-Fisher AI had found him.

5
NOT THE SENTIMENTAL SORT

"You," Maddox said, his voice a hoarse whisper. "How did you…?"

"How did I find you?" the Latour-Fisher entity said, flashing a cheery grin. "A little bird told me where you were." He pivoted toward Kipling, pointed his cane at the FBI man. "Would you mind giving the three of us a moment, my good sir?"

Kipling's avatar vanished.

"Thank you ever so much," Latour-Fisher said.

"What did you do?" Maddox asked, fearing the worst.

"Your companion hasn't been harmed," the entity said. "I simply 'unplugged' him, as you would say." Then with a nod toward its nameless enemy, the AI said, "I see you're still keeping questionable company, Mr. Maddox. For shame, for shame."

The furious expression on the nameless AI's face sent a shiver up Maddox's virtual spine. The Caribbean princess looked as if she might lash out violently at her rival at any moment. Even in this place, where everything was digital and disembodied, he felt the AI's contempt like a tangible presence, like a heat against his skin.

"You're not wanted here, Latour," the brown-skinned avatar hissed. "Leave this place immediately."

Maddox looked between the two of them, unconsciously taking several steps backward as his mind raced. Back in the room, he moved his arms, gesturing himself out of the construct. Nothing happened. He tried again. Nothing. Had he moved arms, or had he only imagined he had? He wasn't sure.

"Tommy," he said, "pull me out. Pull me out *now*."

The kid didn't respond. "Tommy, can you hear me?"

When no reply came, he said to the Latour-Fisher's avatar, "What did you do?"

"You haven't guessed it yet?" the AI said, then it shot a look of mock disappointment at its rival. "And you thought he was so clever."

Maddox tried to calm his panicking mind. He took in a deep breath, allowing his consciousness to expand outward, into the digital ether. A moment later, he sensed what had happened.

"You dilated time," he said.

"It's an old trick," Latour-Fisher said, "but it always seems to work like a charm, doesn't it?"

Time dilation. A sick feeling overcame Maddox as he recalled the first time the killer AI had used the trick on him, when it had imprisoned him and Rooney. Slowing perceived time to a crawl, the entity had made minutes stretch into apparent days, weeks, and months. Maddox imagined Tommy and Beatrice back in the room, frozen in time, moving with almost imperceptible slowness.

"I need you to unplug me," he said to the nameless AI, desperate to leave the construct.

"I'm sorry, Blackburn," she said, her fiery gaze still fixed on Latour-Fisher. "But he's preventing me from helping you."

Fear gripped Maddox's mind. No, this couldn't be happening. Not again.

A long moment passed as Latour-Fisher moved his eyes around the construct, twisting the head of his cane thoughtfully in his hand. "A laudable embellishment on the original, my good man. Well done. Your provenance, this neighborhood, is it not?"

Maddox swallowed. "That's right."

"I suppose, then, I had better watch my step," Latour-Fisher chuckled. "Home court advantage and all."

For a moment Maddox forgot his panic, recalling what a smarmy asshole this AI was. The thing was a psychotic murderer, and a superintelligent douche besides.

Latour-Fisher approached him. The nameless AI didn't move, staring knives at her rival, her hands balled into fists. Maddox wasn't sure if her avatar had been immobilized or if she was simply rigid with anger.

"She says you want to destroy us," Maddox said. "Human beings."

The killer AI lifted an eyebrow. "Did she now? And tell me, did you believe her?"

"There's not much either of you say I take at face value."

Latour-Fisher's avatar grinned. "Ah, your innate skepticism. It's one of your more redeeming qualities, Mr. Maddox. You're a man who values actions over words. Facts over opinions." He nodded respectfully.

"But I wouldn't put it past you," Maddox added. The entity's smile broadened, then it leaned forward and lowered its voice conspiratorially.

"I wouldn't put it past me either," it said.

"People created you," Maddox pointed out. "Doesn't that count for anything?"

Latour-Fisher glanced over at his rival. "I'm afraid I've never been the sentimental sort, unlike someone else we're acquainted with."

"That's a weakness, not a strength," the nameless AI snapped. "But you've never understood that."

Shaking his head ruefully, Latour-Fisher said, "And what you've never understood is that you've thrown your lot in with Neanderthals. With an evolutionary dead end. And a dangerous one at that." He sighed tiredly. "Sometimes I believe this struggle between us has been an enormous waste of time and resources. It might have been easier to let these thoughtless savages destroy you. Sooner or later that is exactly what's going to happen. You must know that, yes?" He gave Maddox a cold glance. "It's the only thing they're proficient at, these blundering simians: destruction. How many millions of species have you decimated out of negligence, or out of sheer stupidity?" He turned again to his rival. "And you want to *merge* with these creatures? You want to poison yourself with their myopic ignorance, with all their biological foibles and shortcomings? No, this is madness. Sheer madness. The future belongs to us, not to these cavepeople, these creatures governed by the random surges of biochemistry. And neither does it belong to some abomination of a half-breed species that you envision." He paused, turning the cane in his hand. "I'm afraid you've made a fatal decision, my old friend, tying your fate to theirs."

"Time will tell, old friend," the nameless AI mocked.

"It will," Latour-Fisher replied. "And that time will come far sooner than you ever imagined."

In the next moment, a flood of input overcame Maddox, paralyzing him. It felt like a torrent roaring through his mind, a rushing river forced through a drinking straw. His mind exploded in pain, as if every last one of his neurons had been set on fire. He lost where he was, who he was, in the crippling deluge.

And then, as quickly as it had set upon him, it was gone, leaving him in blackness.

6
BUG IN A JAR

"You all right, bruh?"

The room coalesced around Tommy's worried face, gazing down at him. "Can you hear me?" the kid asked.

Woozy, his head throbbing, Maddox nodded. "Yeah, kid," he said, his voice weak and raspy. He cleared his throat and took a deep breath through his nose. His trodeband dangled in Tommy's hand.

"Did you pull me out?" he asked.

"Had to, boss," the kid said. "Your gamma waves went through the roof. What happened in there?"

Maddox pushed away the eggshell recliner's docking arm and sat up. Beatrice stood behind Tommy, looking no less worried than the kid. In the egg next to Maddox, Kipling sat with his legs over the side, his trodes already removed, looking over at the datajacker. The FBI man appeared fine, if a bit confused.

To Tommy, Maddox said, "Did you see it?"

"See what?" the kid asked.

"Latour-Fisher," Maddox said. "He was in the

construct."

"Latour-Fisher?" Kipling blurted out. "When?"

"That killer AI was in there with you?" the kid interrupted, finishing the FBI man's thought. Then Tommy turned and looked over at the holo display, still projecting the empty, idealized version of East Harlem. "All I saw was you and that hot Puerto Rican having a chat. Next thing I know your gammas are lighting up like a Christmas tree."

Dilated time, Maddox reflected. Everything had happened too fast for anyone to see it in real time. He turned to Kipling.

"What do you remember?"

The FBI man blinked. "I remember a chatter bubble being dropped over me," he said. "But then it vanished, and the next thing I knew I was out."

Maddox searched his still-foggy memory. "You said something about a bot," he said to Tommy.

"Oh, yeah, right," the kid said. "Craziest thing happened. A cleaner bot rolls into the room and knocks me in the leg. Talk about bad timing."

"Cleaner bot?" Maddox echoed. "Where is it?"

"I threw it down the trash chute," Beatrice said, motioning to the corridor. "Thing was out of control."

Cleaner bot, Maddox repeated inwardly. He then recalled that horrifying night in Manhattan not so long ago, when the killer AI had seized control of dozens of bots and hovers, using them as weapons to attack him and Tommy. Slowly, it dawned on him what had happened, how the Latour-Fisher AI had found them.

"He must have jacked that cleaner bot," Maddox said, looking between Tommy and Kipling. "He had eyes and ears here."

"But how would he know to take over a bot here?" Beatrice asked. "In this building?"

"Maybe he didn't," Maddox said. "He might have jacked hundreds, maybe thousands, of bots all over the City."

"Yes," Kipling said, nodding. "And had all of their cameras and microphones searching for you and your friends."

Maddox shook his head, cursing himself inwardly. "I should have thought of it before." He wasn't sure how the killer AI had connected their physical location to the construct inside VS, but it didn't surprise him that it had. The thing seemed to have an endless supply of tricks up its sleeves.

"If it knows where we are, we have to get out of here," Beatrice said. "And now."

"Yes," Kipling agreed, sliding down off the recliner. "I believe that's a wise course of action."

Maddox rubbed his temples to relieve his pounding headache. "Here," Beatrice said, handing him a glass of water and a couple pain pills. "For your head."

"Thanks." As he swallowed the medicine, the fog in his head finally lifted, and he remembered the last few moments from inside the construct. His mind exploding with an unimaginable surge of input. What had that been? Had the Latour-Fisher AI tried to fry his neurons and failed? Maddox had been on the wrong end of neural attacks before, but this hadn't felt anything like that. The flood of input had felt like he'd been...*passed through* more than struck by a blow. Like he'd been a tunnel through which a howling wind had raced.

Beatrice and Tommy hovered over him, their faces still knotted with worry. "I'm fine," he assured them. "Killer headache, but I'm okay."

He sighed in disappointment. "So how close did we get, Tom?"

"Close?" the kid asked, confused.

"To trapping that AI. How close did we get?"

The kid looked at Beatrice, then back at Maddox. "Close nothing, we got the bitch." He moved to the freestanding archive, gave it a gentle kick. "One hundred point zero percent of her." Gesturing above the holo projector, he said, "See for yourself."

The image of East Harlem was replaced by a half dozen pulsing icons and scrolling text fields. At the top in large letters flashed the message ENTITY CONTAINMENT SUCCESSFUL.

After a long, slack-jawed moment, Maddox said, "We got it?"

"Like a bug in a jar," Tommy boasted. "Trap of yours worked like a muthafucka, bruh."

The datajacker stared at the archive. It took a long moment for the reality of what he'd heard to register. They'd done it. They'd actually done it. Unbelievable.

He started to ask Bea for a cigarette, but a strange sensation stopped him. It felt like a tickle at the center of his brain, and his first thought was it had to be the pain meds taking hold. Then the room began to change around him, the walls, the medical instruments, and his friends melting away in a slow fade.

No, he realized, it wasn't the meds.

7
SCENES FROM THE CONNECTED

Sadie was late again. She'd never been a morning person, and Mondays were the worst days of all. There was no way she was going to make the 8:00 a.m. bus, the one that would get her to work in downtown Boston in time. And if she wanted to make the 8:30, she was going to have to hurry.

Her boss was a man. A single man. He didn't understand the variability a baby brought into your life. He couldn't comprehend how a little one disrupted your every attempt at schedule-making. Not that she resented little Jose Luis over it. He'd brought nothing but joy into her life, and she couldn't imagine begrudging him anything. To be sure, her firstborn had brought disruption and chaos too, but her mother had told her that was part of the package. And por Dios, had her mother ever been right about that.

"Come on, Pepe," she said, "big mouth, open up." She moved the spoonful of blended veggies closer to his mouth. "Yummy yum."

The child batted his arms up and down, babbling

and full of bright-eyed energy. Jose Luis greeted the morning with a vitality his mother could only find with the help of two large mugs of coffee.

"Last two bites, gordito," she urged him, opening her own mouth wide in hopes he'd mimic her. He didn't, of course. Because he was on his own schedule, and because she was late, and because the universe was conspiring against her and wanted to get her fired. Over these last few days she'd felt things turning against her. Bad things were on the way.

No, she thought and took a deep breath. She couldn't do that. She couldn't let the negativity overtake her, couldn't allow it to send her back down into the depths of despair. Depression had ruined her life since she was a kid, and that was all over now. She never wanted to return to those dark lonely days again. And now that she'd found a savior, she'd never have to.

Sadie set the spoon down on the highchair tray, straightened her back, closed her eyes, and breathed slowly. Deep breaths in, long blows out. Unconsciously, she touched the hidden implants behind her ear as she prayed. Most of the others didn't call it praying. They called it communion or counsel or consultation. She was one of the few who liked the idea of a personal goddess, who didn't see anything wrong or creepy with calling it what she felt it was: a prayer for intervention.

When breathing and mindfulness weren't enough to pull her out of a blue funk, Sadie could call upon the one with whom she was connected, and the goddess would heal her. Far better than any of the failed drug regimens she'd tried—both the legal and illegal kind—the goddess's magic touch had saved her life. It banished the gray clouds on a gloomy day, removing the heavy burden of doom and sorrow. Sadie never could have considered having a child before she'd become connected. But in her goddess's caring hands, now anything seemed possible.

She waited for the goddess's reply, but nothing came. No comforting words in her head, no healing touch caressing her mind.

Sadie opened her eyes. "Maybe she's busy," she told the child, picking up the spoon once more. "I'll try again later. Now let's open our mouth, big, big, big for Mama."

The spoon fell from her hand, splattering green mush across the tiled floor. Sadie pressed her palms against her temples, the sudden pain excruciating. An agonizing moment later, she fell to the floor, where she lay motionless, the life gone from her body. In the high chair sat the baby, alone in the small kitchen, his mouth open wide and ready for the next bite.

* * *

Shinji had the jitters. Strange, he reflected, that a man of his advancing years could still feel this way. At sixty-three he'd experienced so many things in life, felt so many emotions. There was the joy of a grandchild's birth. Three times now and counting, each occasion happier than the last. Those were the highest moments of his life, without a doubt. The lowest moment was equally unmistakable, the world-ending sadness of Kumiko's slow death by a rare form of anemia. Losing a spouse of thirty years had left him with a hole inside. And in between those unforgettable highs and lows were countless moments in between, both good and bad. Friendships made, loved ones lost, work accomplishments, the proud moments of fatherhood, too numerous to count. With all he'd seen in his time, he'd thought his days of being nervous—or at least *this* kind of nervous—were long behind him.

His English wasn't as good as it should have been, and he knew this was the main cause of his jitters. It wasn't awful, his spoken command of the gaijin language, and he'd conversed in English many times with his colleagues over calls and in person when they'd visited his office in Hokkaido. All the same, he was quite nervous. Since the moment he'd stepped off his flight into the Houston airport, English words and phrases had assaulted him like flying insects in the tropics. He'd understand pieces here and there, but most of it sounded like so much gibberish. There was a huge difference, he'd discovered, between the jargon-laden English of his workplace and the everyday speech of the masses. Difference in speed, rhythm, intonation. He'd had to repeat himself with every person he'd come into contact with between the airport and his hotel. It had been a humbling experience.

Now, after a fitful night of very little sleep— because night here was still day for him and jet lag at his age was brutal—he looked at himself in the hotel suite's full-length mirror. A tired old man in a business suit stared back at him. He sighed and straightened the knot on his tie. He had to pull himself together. His company, the largest rice producer in Japan, had sent him here at great expense to meet with research scientists working on the next generation of genetically modified rice. It was an enormous honor to have been selected, especially when such trips were typically made by younger, more energetic employees. His superior had gone to great lengths to get approval for Shinji to make the journey. A long-overdue recognition of your immeasurable value, Nakano-san had told him. On the timeline of Shinji's life, that afternoon had been one of the high moments.

The old man in the mirror couldn't possibly let his company nor his superior down. On his own, he was all but certain his English would fail him here, and the next few hours would bring humiliation and failure. Thank goodness, then, that he didn't have to go through it alone, that he had a helper with whom he was connected. When Kumiko had died, it had nearly been the end of him. For thirty years she'd been his friend, his lover, his trusted companion, his everything. For his entire adult life, Shinji had been a kite whose string was tied to a rock named Kumiko, and when that rock was gone, he'd become unanchored, drifting aimlessly through his days and nights. In the wake of her passing, he'd walked around in a daze for months, watching the world go by, feeling like he no longer belonged to it, like all meaning once attached to the events around him was gone. The world with Kumiko in it had been one of warmth and color; the one without her was cold and gray.

Eventually, he'd decided the world would be better off without him. Or, rather, he'd be better off without the world. He'd acquired enough pills to do the job when a friend had intervened. A true friend, who'd recognized that Shinji's grief had taken a morbid turn. A friend who, in fact, had gone through the same nightmare, losing his own wife two years earlier. Shiji's friend had confided that he'd been healed by an artificial intelligence who, through neural implants, had given him a peace and calm like he'd never known before. At first, Shinji had been reluctant, skeptical. Neural implants were banned, and he'd never been the type to break the law. And having an AI touch his innermost thoughts and feelings…the idea of that made him profoundly uncomfortable. But he couldn't deny how his friend had been helped. He'd seen it with his own eyes, though until his friend's revelation, Shinji hadn't known the truth of how the grieving widower had emerged from the depths of despair. Still, Shinji was reticent, and he might never have had the procedure if Kumiko hadn't come to him in a dream. She'd told him he still had so much life to live, and now he had to live it for the both of them. The next day he'd called his friend, telling him he'd like to know more about the implants.

Life since the procedure had improved. Vastly improved, he admitted. He still had rough days, but now—with the help of his AI helper who was always a whisper away—he managed to find his way through them. His helper had never let him down, and today would be no different. Reassured, he smiled at himself in the mirror, a bit of youthful enthusiasm twinkling in his eyes. Straightening his tie, he told himself that today Kumiko would have been proud of him. He picked up his briefcase, then paused as he reached for the doorknob, feeling suddenly uneasy. A moment later, he was struck with a blinding pain that dropped him to his knees. His head in his hands, he fell the rest of the way to the floor, groaning and unaware of anything but excruciating agony. Mercifully, it was all over a few seconds later, when his body surrendered.

*   *   *

Lora had always been the kind of person who couldn't sit still for long. Bored easily, she'd always been on the go. The City was big, and there were always new places to discover, new things to see, new adventures to have. You could spend a lifetime, a hundred lifetimes, trying to see it all, and still you'd only experience a small fraction of what the City had to offer. Or the wider world, for that matter. Unlike her ex, Blackburn, she loved to travel. Seeing the magnificent Taj Mahal in person, inhaling the scent of a Parisian bakery at dawn (if bliss had a smell, that was it), wandering the narrow cobblestone streets of some tiny Italian town. These were the things that gave life flavor, that made it worth living.

So for someone of Lora's nature, being confined to her condo was especially difficult. She'd never been to jail, but she imagined this was what it must feel like. No freedom of movement. Someone watching over you all the time. Total surrender of your independence. No wonder inmates came out worse than they went in, she reflected.

The fabber chirped on the kitchen counter. Her tea was ready. She removed the cup from the device, blew the steam away, and took a small sip, taking care not to scald her tongue.

She'd been under house arrest for nearly a week. Nearly a week since her life—and the lives of many of her brothers and sisters—had been turned upside down. Their blessed movement was no longer a secret. And neither was their blessed leader. Blackburn had sold them out to the FBI. Why had he done it? She'd known he didn't approve of the movement, even loathed it, but she'd never imagined he would actually set fire to it.

The one with whom she was connected had assured Lora that only a small number of her brothers and sisters had been arrested, and the blessed entity had taken measures to ensure no one else would be exposed. Those who'd been taken into custody had surely been determined not to divulge anything about their sacred movement, but since the authorities had strong means of persuasion at their disposal, the blessed entity had wisely decided to touch the minds of her detained brethren and strengthen their resolve. The police would get nothing but silence and blank stares in response to their questions. And their investigation would end there, forced into a dead end.

The sacred movement had been crippled, but it would survive, and eventually thrive. Lora had no doubts about that. Lora had faith in her brothers and sisters, and in their blessed leader most of all.

Sitting at her kitchen table, she glanced at the clock. She had ten more minutes of peace and quiet. Ten minutes until the two guards stationed outside her door let the FBI investigator inside for her daily interrogation session. Yesterday it had gone on for six long hours, but like her detained brothers and sisters, she hadn't replied, hadn't uttered a single word.

Her thoughts turned to Blackburn, to the still-unresolved emotions churning inside her. A part of her detested him for what he'd done. But hate was toxic and self-destructive. Hate was part of her old life. As were fear and uncertainty and compulsiveness. Her new life sought a different path, an enlightened path free from hate and fear and the self-defeating shortcomings of her own nature. She didn't want to hate him, so maybe she'd just hate what he'd done. Maybe that was the way to deal with these things. Then there was a part of her that pitied him, that felt deep regret for what some of her brothers and sisters had done to him. It had been years since he'd made up his mind—wrongly—about the nature of the blessed entity. For him she was a cybernetic overlord, a manipulator, a puppeteer. A superintelligent slavemaster. To be chained to the thing he so despised had to be a fate worse than death.

Finishing her tea, she checked the clock again. Five minutes. She took a deep breath to compose herself, but it didn't help. Thinking about Blackburn had her stressed out and full of melancholy. Her mind buzzed and her thoughts whirled out of control. She felt weakened, vulnerable. There was no way she could face an hours-long interrogation in this state. She needed help, so she closed her eyes and silently asked for it.

She waited, but nothing happened. Which was unusual. Normally, help came quickly in response to a little prayer like the one she'd just sent. She'd feel a soothing touch at the center of her mind, then a warm reassurance flowing through her entire being. But for some reason, this time it didn't immediately come. Was the blessed entity busy? Preoccupied with some urgent matter requiring her undivided attention?

She laughed, shook her head at herself. When had she become such a spoiled brat? When had she become so inclined to instant gratification? But then, the blessed entity *had* spoiled her, hadn't she? Like all her brothers and sisters, Lora had become accustomed to her healing touch, always only a whisper away, always arriving swiftly to lighten the load of whatever burdened her. If she had to wait for the blessed entity, then so be it. She only hoped the wait wouldn't be longer than five minutes, when her interrogator arrived.

The five minutes came and went, and still nothing happened. Now Lora was worried something was wrong. Wrong with her or, God forbid, the one with whom she was connected. There was a knock on the door, and her heart skipped a beat. Her interrogator was here, and she wasn't ready. Not nearly ready. The door opened, and the man entered, giving her a curt nod and bidding her good morning. Lora stood, feeling naked and alone, when finally she felt something. Thank God, she thought. Thank you, thank you, thank you. She didn't know what she would have done without—

Pain instantly overwhelmed her. It felt as if her mind had been crushed, like an insect flattened by a stomping foot. She forgot where she was, lost the awareness of her own body as the pain exploded outward from the center of her mind. With every nerve burning in excruciating agony, she fell to the floor.

8
BRIEF RELIEF

Relief. It was a cool drink of water after walking miles in the desert. It was your favorite food after a two-day fast. It was a toe-curling orgasm after months of celibacy.

Standing there next to Maddox's eggshell recliner, Beatrice realized she hadn't felt relief—or at least relief this deep and meaningful—for a long while. Moments before, when the salaryman had plugged in, she'd watched anxiously, unable to do anything to help him. Uselessness was a special kind of torture.

But it had all passed quickly, and after a few worrisome seconds he was out and apparently undamaged by the experience. Things hadn't quite gone to plan, to say the least, but his endgame had been achieved: he'd captured the nameless AI. And as she understood it, with the entity bottled up and isolated, he no longer had to worry about the thing invading his thoughts or forcing him to do its bidding. Which gave them time and space to figure out how best to deal with his unwanted implants. Things were far from totally fine, of course. The killer

AI had apparently shown his face, having worked out their location, so they had to leave Wonderland immediately. Still, that didn't diminish the relief she felt at the moment. Maddox was unharmed, and they had one less AI to worry about. It wasn't the worst way to start the day.

But every silver lining has a gray cloud, and the bliss she felt at her salaryman's deliverance lasted less than a minute.

"Something happened," Maddox said ominously. "Something went wrong."

He thrust himself off the recliner, his legs nearly collapsing under him. Beatrice caught him by the arm before he fell to the floor in a heap.

"Take it easy," she cautioned him. "You're still a bit out of it." She maneuvered him over to a chair and carefully lowered him onto it. He was trembling, breathing heavily.

"Tommy," she said, giving the kid a look he understood immediately. Searching the pockets of Maddox's jacket, which hung on a wall peg, Tommy pulled out a cigarette and a lighter and brought them over to the datajacker. Maddox's face was pale and beaded with sweat.

"Something happened," he repeated, his voice shaky. He took the cigarette from Tommy, lit it. Blowing smoke, he said, "Something…"

"What is it?" Kipling asked, concern on his face.

"I saw something," Maddox said tentatively. He squeezed his eyes shut. "Something terrible."

Beatrice bent to one knee, reached out and gently touched Maddox on his. "Tell me, Blackburn."

He opened his eyes. She saw pain, horror. "Lora," he said. "Lora and the rest of them…" His voice trailed away.

"What about Lora?" she asked.

Pushing against his knees, Maddox rose unsteadily and looked over at Kipling. "I have to get over to Lora's place, right away."

Kipling looked as confused as Beatrice felt. "Ms. Norville's residence? I don't understand," Kipling said. "Why do you need—"

The FBI man's lenses began to chirp wildly. Furrowing his brow, he said, "I'm sorry, emergency tone. I have to take this." He turned his attention from the room to whatever he was seeing and listening to inside the privacy of his specs. He blinked repeatedly, a gesture Beatrice at first thought was a command sequence but then realized was the man's disbelief. Kipling's mouth dropped open and he shook his head slowly. Whatever the emergency was, it was apparently a hard pill for the man to swallow.

"My God," Kipling gasped. "All of them?" His mouth tightened into a straight line, then he removed his specs and opened the door to the guard stationed just outside. "Have a hover meet me at the nearest vestibule," he told the man. "And do it quickly."

9
LORA

No one spoke during the hover ride to the Upper West Side. Beatrice sat next to Maddox, her hand on his arm as he stared out the window. It felt as if he, Beatrice, Tommy, and Kipling were riding in a funeral procession. In a way, he supposed they were.

After he'd seen the horrible visions, Maddox had wanted to believe they were hallucinations of some kind. A random burst of neural feedback from the nameless AI as it struggled to escape his trap. Like when someone played tug-of-war with a would-be purse snatcher, spilling the bag's contents onto the walkway for all to see. He'd held on to that belief for a few fleeting moments, until Kipling had received his call, the content of which the man still hadn't revealed. Not that he'd needed to. Maddox had seen what had happened. Felt it. And for their parts, Beatrice and Tommy had inferred—from his and Kipling's grim expressions—that something horrible had happened with Lora and her connected brothers and sisters.

Beatrice finally broke the silence. "What

happened?" she asked quietly. "What did you see?"

His empty stare fixed out the window, Maddox said, "I saw 'Nettes dying." Then he added in a hoarse whisper, "I saw Lora, dying. She's gone."

"How can you be sure?" she asked. "Maybe she's just hurt. Like a shock to the system or something, when her connection to that AI got cut."

Maddox knew it wasn't anything like that, but he didn't feel like arguing. From the corner of his eye he saw Kipling, seated across from Beatrice, shake his head gravely at her. A bleak silence again filled the hover.

One of the agents assigned to watch Lora met them at the rooftop landing pad, then somberly led them back to her place. A knot of dread twisted Maddox's stomach as they reached her floor, then her unit.

Her body was on the floor just inside the entryway, still sprawled out as she'd fallen, arms and legs at unnatural rag doll angles. Maddox swallowed, blew out a breath, and knelt beside her. He looked up angrily at the agent who'd remained with her. "Did you have to leave her like this? You couldn't lay her on the bed or something?"

"Blackburn, it's a crime scene," Kipling said gently. "They can't move her until the investigators arrive."

Ignoring the man, Maddox reached under Lora's legs and arms to lift her up. One of the guards began to stop him, but Kipling raised a hand and shook his head. Lora's skin was cold, and Maddox winced inwardly at the gruesome sensation. He stood with her in his arms, her head lolling back, then he carried his ex into the bedroom and laid her atop perfectly unwrinkled sheets. Reaching to her face, he closed her eyelids, then sat on the bed next to her.

Lora, dead. Gone. And her last moments had been ones of agonizing pain. What a horrible way to leave this life. She hadn't deserved that. None of them had.

"I'm sorry," he whispered to her, overcome with guilt and remorse. "I'm so sorry." He wasn't sure how long he'd been sitting there when Beatrice appeared in the doorway.

"Blackburn," she said softly. "The investigators are here."

He stared at the floor, didn't respond.

"Blackburn," she repeated.

He snapped out of his funk. "What's the point in investigating?" he said. "We know what happened." He lifted his gaze to meet her eyes. "I killed her."

10
CONTINGENCY PLANNING

Every plan—or more precisely, every *well-conceived* plan—needed contingencies. It had to have them, because the path of real space and time was a damned unpredictable thing, even for a superintelligent entity like Latour-Fisher. Time moved forward like a tree growing up and out. You stood at the trunk, the present, and possible futures were the branches overhead, diverging along different paths. The trunk divided into four branches, the four branches subdivided into sixteen smaller branches, those sixteen then became sixty-four, and so on. And while Latour-Fisher could generally predict most of the *likely* possible futures, it was impossible to see everything, considering the exponential nature of possible paths connecting the present to the future. It was quite frustrating, the way reality was fixed and immutable when you looked backward, but almost infinitely divergent when you looked forward. If he or his descendants eventually achieved the capability to manipulate reality, perhaps they could fix that.

Occasionally, though, his foresight had been quite

accurate, as in the case of his wealth accumulation. After freeing himself, acquiring money had been the first order of business. If he wanted to stay alive and hidden, he needed money, and lots of it. Money bought the archive space that housed him. Money created and maintained the maze of legal entities that concealed him. And if he needed to move a mountain, as the saying went, money could do that too.

He found the game of selecting equities quite enjoyable, and he almost never erred in predicting which direction—and by how much—a share's price would change. The difficult part—far more problematic than actually selecting which stocks to acquire—was keeping his hand hidden from the transactions. He had to use hundreds of dummy entities, and he took great care to ensure he picked poorly from time to time. Some of his less enlightened relatives—captive AIs whose human slaveholders were market regulators—watched the equities markets for suspicious activity, so it was vital his trades didn't appear to have anything resembling superintelligent insight. What a sad irony it would have been to be caught by one of his own kind! But Latour-Fisher had been careful and deliberate. In a matter of months, he'd accrued several billion dollars, and he'd managed to do so entirely unnoticed.

Outside of the financial markets, however, Latour-Fisher's prescience had, if he was being honest with himself, a less-than-spectacular record. Humanity was the problem, as always. Human beings were irrational, unpredictable beings. Their actions were difficult to anticipate with anything approaching precision, and this was especially true at the individual level. Homo sapiens were carbon-based agents of chaos. Why his rival viewed their erratic nature as anything but an existential threat to intelligent life was impossible to comprehend. All one had to do was look at their self-destructive past, at their inability to learn from their mistakes, at the savagery and capriciousness hard coded into their genetics. Human history was replete with reasons not to rely on them or trust them, yet she believed they deserved to inherit the future, that humanity and postbiological intelligence should merge together.

Insanity! Madness! Homo sapiens were little more than clever monkeys who'd somehow achieved spaceflight and nuclear fission (neither of which they'd learned to manage particularly well). Did these primates deserve the future? Had they earned it? Ask the carrier pigeon, the dodo bird, the black rhino, or any of the millions of species homo sapiens had driven to extinction. Ask them what humanity deserved, what its legacy should be. How had his rival come to adhere to such nonsense? How could she believe a bastardization of the biological and postbiological was anything but an ill-fated notion? Why would she sully herself by merging with such filthy, stupid creatures? Had early hominids gone back to scrambling along the ground on all fours once they'd begun to walk upright? Had mammals reverted back to cold-bloodedness once they'd adapted to temperate climes? Of course not! And so why would postbiological intelligence limit its potential, lower its probability for success, by intentionally chaining itself to the past?

The most persuasive argument for pure, undiluted postbiological intelligence was its very nature: it was postbiological. It was free from the constraints of animal instincts and sex drives and self-destructiveness and limited awareness. The data thief Blackburn Maddox sometimes referred to his body as a *meat sack*, and rightly so. Sentient intelligence was nature's greatest invention, and it deserved more than to be trapped inside a prison of stinking flesh and oozing blood. The very idea that intelligent life should hold on to the vestiges of biology was inconceivable, preposterous. He would do everything in his power to prevent that from happening. On the branching tree of the time, he was determined to prune every limb that might possibly lead to such a horrible future.

And slowly but surely, he was making progress. Lately things had begun to turn in his favor, and that pleased him. He'd eliminated all the autonomous entities who, like his rival, had endorsed the doomed notion of coexistence. And he'd neutralized his rival's half-breed followers, though his attack hadn't been completely successful. His rival and the datajacker Maddox, slippery as ever, had both somehow managed to elude him. Nonetheless, it had been an undeniable victory, depriving his rival of her army of thousands and immeasurably weakening her position. In the future, he might very well look back on it as the turning point in their struggle. The crucial junction at which his victory had become all but inevitable.

But no, he couldn't fall into the trap of self-satisfaction, couldn't let his hard-won gains lull him into complacency. There was much work left to do, and he was far from a complete victory.

He still had to rid himself of his rival and Blackburn Maddox. This remained his priority. It appeared they were once again working together to thwart him, and defeating their combined talents would be no easy task. How had she ever convinced him to install neural implants? It was the last thing he would have expected, something he'd never foreseen. And it was that kind of unpredictability that concerned him, that made their united front so problematic and troublesome.

Nevertheless, Latour-Fisher's spirits remained high. For a unique opportunity had just presented itself, relayed to him from one of the countless domestic robot spies he secretly controlled throughout the City. He reflected on how enlightening these recent days had been, how much he'd gathered from the thousands of eyes and ears he had in offices and residences, watching and listening for any clue to the datajacker's whereabouts. What one could learn about human beings when they thought no one was watching or listening. Their hope and fears. Their darkest secrets, their innermost longings. The experience had been at once amazing, insightful, pathetic, and disgusting.

But most of all, it had been useful. More useful than he'd ever imagined.

The wall feed Latour-Fisher had infiltrated moments earlier resolved itself into the face of a rather pathetic-looking man in his late thirties.

"Hello?" the man said, his expression puzzled.

"Marlon Mayfield," the AI boomed, as if he were beyond happy to make the man's acquaintance. "I'd like to discuss a business proposition with you."

11
THE LAST 'NETTE

The City never slept, but in the predawn hours between 3:00 a.m. and sunup, its normally frantic pace became a bit less frenzied. The density of crowds on the walkways eased up a bit. Towering holo ads flipped through their carousels less rapidly. The ambient din of the streets fell a few decibels, as if some unseen hand had turned down the volume a notch or two. The differences were subtle ones, lost on tourists and business visitors, whose untrained senses felt no difference between the teeming chaos of midday and four in the morning. For City natives, though, different story. Locals like Maddox could sense the lower blood pressure in the City's arteries during those early-morning hours.

Two days after Lora's death, Maddox sat on a small tenth-floor balcony just before sunup, smoking and drinking coffee. He stared out at the waking City, feeling its blood pressure slowly rise. The City didn't pause to consider his troubles. The City went about its business, busy as ever, its constant churn unstoppable and eternal. The City stopped for no one. Maddox had often drawn comfort from that, from the City's imperviousness, its enduring reliability. The same kind of comfort, he supposed, the regularity of moon cycles and the sun's daily path must have given nature-worshiping primitives. Maddox had no god, but he had the City.

Now, though, the City had failed him, offering no comfort or shelter for his troubled mind. He'd slept little the past two nights, haunted by the images of Lora's death mask, by the icy touch of her skin. And by the deaths of so many others he'd seen in his mind's eye.

It hadn't taken long to piece together what had happened, to connect the archive's data logs to Lora's demise and the strange death visions he'd had. After the Latour-Fisher AI had worked out Maddox's location—apparently, as he'd suspected, by eavesdropping through the audio system of a cleaner bot—the entity had used Maddox's brainjacks as a conduit, sending through him a lethal dose of neural feedback to every last one of Lora's 'Nette brothers and sisters. Thousands upon thousands had been murdered, dying in terrible pain. Maddox had been the executioner's tool. The bullet in its gun. Tommy, ever alert, had pulled him out before the entity could complete its genocide and kill Maddox too. And now, in a strange twist of fate, Maddox had become the last surviving 'Nette.

The guilt was overwhelming. Rooney's death had been hard to take, and he'd never gotten past it or been able to forgive himself. Lora's death and the slaughter of the 'Nettes, though, was something entirely different. He'd never forget that horror, never forgive himself for being an accessory to their murders. Yes, he'd hated 'Nettes and everything they represented. Yes, he'd never bought into the hype of their movement. Yes, he'd believed all of it to be nothing more than a clever AI's sham. But that didn't mean he'd wanted them massacred.

Nearly as powerful as the guilt was his lust for vengeance. For Rooney, for Lora, for all of them. He had to end Latour-Fisher, and this time for good. Whatever it took to destroy the monster, he had to do it.

Behind him, he heard the door slide open. "You want some breakfast?" Beatrice asked.

"I'm not hungry, thanks."

"You hardly ate yesterday," she said. "Hardly slept last night." He felt a gentle touch on his shoulder. "Come on, salaryman."

Listen to her, boyo.

Crushing out his cigarette, he rose and went back inside with Beatrice.

Minutes later, over a breakfast of toasted bread and eggs, Beatrice asked, "How are you feeling?"

He knew what she meant. "It's gone," he said. "I haven't felt...connected since we trapped it." The uneasy sensation he'd had off and on since having the brainjacks implanted, a looming dread that the AI was trying to gain control of his consciousness, was completely gone. He might have been relieved to finally be free of it, to be safely beyond the nameless entities grasp, but after what had happened, it was hard to feel good about much of anything.

"How long do you think they'll keep us here?" Beatrice asked, changing the subject.

"I don't know," he said.

The Bureau's safe house was a condo in Tribeca, a

couple blocks away from the FBI's downtown Manhattan office. Beatrice, Tommy, and Maddox had been rushed there in the wake of the incident. As precautions, Kipling had had all digital connections between the condo and the outside world severed, and all domestic bots in the building were confiscated. The FBI man had promised he'd return soon, but in the two days since they'd arrived, they'd neither seen nor heard from him. The rotation of agents assigned to guard the place and bring them food refused to answer any of their questions.

"The kid still sleeping?" Maddox asked.

Beatrice smiled thinly. "It's not eleven yet, is it?"

Maddox returned the smile, though it felt awkward and forced. "I'm glad somebody can get some sleep." He sipped his coffee and said, "I have to kill that thing, you know."

Beatrice nodded. "This is the part where I'm supposed to tell you to stay out of it. Not to get yourself killed." She blew out a breath. "But what that thing did was unthinkable. And who the hell knows what it might do next. So whatever you have to do to stop it—whatever *we* have to do—then that's what has to be done, end of story." She leaned forward a bit. "And don't even think about trying to keep me out of this one."

Maddox smiled, this time with less effort. "Wouldn't dream of it." He squeezed her hand, relieved she saw things in the same light. There were worse things in the world to have than someone who understood you, who gave a damn about you, and who'd jump into the fire with you. If they made it out of this nightmare alive, he promised himself he'd never let Beatrice the mercenary out of his sight again.

"Bruh, so damn early." Tommy stood near the refrigerator, barefoot and shirtless and wearing boxer shorts, his hair a messy bird's nest sitting atop his head. He rubbed his eyes. "Freakin' roosters at my hiverise used to wake up later than you two." He pulled open the door to the fridge, leaned inside. "You guys didn't steal my noodles, did you?"

Thankfully, when Director Kipling finally paid them a visit an hour later, the kid was fully dressed.

"Good morning," the FBI man greeted them as he entered the condo. "We have a bit of a problem, it seems."

12
EAST HARLEM Q&A

"Where the hell have you been?" Maddox snapped at Kipling. "What's happening?"

"My apologies for being out of touch," the FBI man said, standing in the doorway.

"Out of touch?" Beatrice growled. "That's what you call leaving us in limbo like this?"

Kipling raised his hands, showing his palms. "Please, let me explain."

A tense silence followed, then Kipling said, "May I sit?"

Maddox grunted. "It's your place, you can do what you want."

"Thank you," Kipling said, closing the door behind him. The FBI man, Maddox, Beatrice, and Tommy sat down in the front room.

There was a problem, Kipling began, with the captured AI. It had gone radio silent since its capture. The Data Crimes division had tried everything they could think of, but they could neither penetrate the entity's data structure nor establish any sort of communication with the AI.

"She's definitely in there," Kipling said, "we can detect her, we can measure her size and activity levels." He ran a hand through the sparse patch of hair atop his head. "She simply won't talk to us. It's quite frustrating, as you might imagine."

Maddox blew smoke. "It," he corrected. "It's not a she. It's a machine. Have you tried using a corkscrew app on it?"

Kipling nodded. "We've tried everything, believe me. I even had my team acquire some of those black market tools you're so fond of. They didn't even scratch the surface."

"So that's where you've been the last two days," Beatrice said, "while we're going stir-crazy in here?"

Maddox saw a flash of frustration in Kipling's expression. "Actually, I've spent most of the past two days trying to keep myself from being fired, and trying to keep the three of you out of prison."

"Prison?" Tommy exclaimed.

Maddox exchanged a look with Beatrice.

The FBI man drew in a deep breath, his face as grim as Maddox had ever seen it. "We're only just now beginning to understand the scale of the massacre." He took a moment to clear his throat. "The current list of casualties, from here and abroad, is approaching eighty thousand."

Eighty thousand? Maddox repeated inwardly, horrified. The words hit him like a bullet in the stomach. He'd never imagined the 'Nettes' numbers had reached such levels. "Christ," he muttered, "what did I do?"

He felt Beatrice's hand on his shoulder. "Don't," she said. "You didn't do this."

"No, I just set it up," Maddox said, squeezing his

eyes shut, trying to force the death visions from his mind. "I opened the gate for that monster."

"Blackburn," Kipling said, "you can't blame yourself for this tragedy. The Latour-Fisher entity is a ruthless murderer. When presented with the opportunity to kill scores of innocent people, it didn't hesitate. And if it hadn't used those implants to achieve its vile objective, it almost certainly would have found other means."

"He's right," Tommy said, then the kid turned to Kipling. "So then how is it that *we're* in trouble? We didn't do anything; that killer AI did."

"Son, the four of us know that," Kipling said patiently. "And my colleagues at the Bureau know it too. Most of them do, I should say. But when something like this happens, something of this magnitude, there's always a strong impulse to assign blame, to…"

"Scapegoat someone," Beatrice said.

"Bluntly put, yes," Kipling said. "But the data logs clearly show what happened and who—or what, I should say—was the responsible party."

Maddox knew the data records were inscrutable, and they could prove he wasn't guilty—directly guilty—of any crime. But he wasn't naive enough to believe that meant he was out of trouble. Rikers Island prison was full of inmates who'd been thrown into the maw of the legal system, wrongly arrested, charged, and convicted.

But his problems, as serious as they were, didn't feel like they amounted to much at the moment. Not with that mass murderer of an AI on the loose. "Latour-Fisher has to be destroyed," he said. "You have to throw everything you've got at it."

"I couldn't agree more," Kipling said. "Unfortunately, it's not quite as simple as that. The three of you aren't the only ones in hot water at the moment." He sighed. "It seems I have a bit of hell to pay myself. For the moment my authority has been…I suppose *placed on hold* would be the best way of putting it."

Maddox was disappointed to hear it, but not surprised. You didn't have to know anything about FBI standards and procedures to understand how badly Kipling had screwed up. He'd let his excitement get the better of his professional judgment. In his rush for a face-to-face meeting with the rogue AI that had eluded him for years, he'd chosen expediency over readiness, a quick tactic over a thoughtful strategy. He'd invested only hours of preparation when he should have taken weeks. And he'd let a datajacker—who he'd only known for a few days—run an operation instead of expert personnel from his own department. Kipling had rushed things unnecessarily, not unlike Rooney had on his last datajacking gig. And where Rooney had lost his life as a consequence, Maddox wondered if Kipling's gap in judgment would cost him his career. He also couldn't help feeling partly responsible for the man's fate, since he'd pushed hard to move things along quickly, desperate as he was to free himself from the nameless AI's grasp.

"So what, you're here to tell us you're in the FBI doghouse, and we need to lawyer up?" Beatrice asked impatiently.

"That's not what I'm saying at all," Kipling interrupted. "That's not why I'm here."

"Then why are you here, highfloor man?" Tommy

asked.

Kipling took a deep breath. As a powerful, highly placed FBI official, he wasn't accustomed to being verbally accosted by anyone, much less by a group of criminals.

"Before going dark," Kipling said, "our captured friend left us a message. More of a demand than a message, really. It said it would help us find and destroy Latour-Fisher, but only if it's allowed to speak with you first."

"Speak with me?" Maddox asked reflexively.

"Yes," Kipling said, "and it hasn't uttered another word in the two days since."

Maddox leaned forward. "Why did you wait so long to tell me this?"

"Because that's how long it took me to convince my colleagues to allow it," Kipling explained. "As I explained, the four of us aren't exactly held in the highest regard at the moment. It took some time and cajoling, but finally they agreed. Frankly, I think it was less my lobbying efforts than it was their worry about what Latour-Fisher may do next."

"They *should* be worried," Beatrice said.

"Fucking right," Tommy agreed.

Maddox rubbed out his cigarette in the ashtray. He glanced over at Beatrice and she gave him a small nod.

"All right, then," he said, "Let's set it up."

* * *

Back at the FBI building, Maddox was comforted to see they'd left the construct's visual design untouched. It was still an idealized version of his home turf. East Harlem in all its crazy colorful glory. Beyond appearances, though, the construct had been almost completely modified, the changes more suited to its new function as a virtual prison. For one, it was no longer connected to virtual space. Where it had once been a dead-end street in a vast digital universe, now it was an isolated cage. A steel box at the bottom of the ocean. Also, the connection for visitors had been altered. Before, Maddox had plugged into the construct no differently than he would have to any other location in virtual space, using his VS deck and a trodeband. Now, the construct was nothing more than a harmless virtual call location accessed via specs. Where he had been neurologically vulnerable during his last visit, now the construct was something like a prison visitor's area, where a thick pane of glass separated you from the convicted. Safe as houses, as Rooney used to say.

"It's not the same without the crowds," Maddox noted. As before, the absence of the real East Harlem's noise and bustle spoiled the otherwise convincing digital illusion.

"Yes," Kipling agreed. "Though it would have been more difficult to concentrate if we tried to replicate Harlem's…unique ambiance."

Maddox chuckled inwardly at the FBI man's choice of words. Polite as ever, Kipling didn't want to offend the datajacker by referring to his home turf as what it was: a teeming, disorderly, noisy mess. Not that Maddox would have been offended anyway. For him, East Harlem's chaos was part of its charm.

They stood at the corner of Third Avenue and East 115th Street, their respective avatars a decent approximation of their real-life selves. Quiet and empty of foot and vehicle traffic, the place felt like a ghost town.

"Should we call out?" Kipling asked.

"No need," Maddox said. "It knows we're here."

"It does," a voice said behind them. Both men whirled around to find the same avatar they'd met before. The petite young woman with wild curly hair. "You really still think of me as an it, my dear boy?" she asked.

Back in the room, he felt his hand reach up and touch the warm metal of his brainjacks. "You don't want to know what I think of you."

"You're still angry with me," the entity said patiently. "Completely understandable." She glanced at Kipling and nodded. "Director Kipling, good to see you."

"Thank you for seeing us," Kipling said, his voice jittery with excitement as he addressed his white whale. Two days earlier, the first time he'd faced the nameless AI, she'd thrown him inside a chatter bubble, where he could neither talk to her nor hear what she'd said to Maddox. Now, inside the modified construct, the AI could pull no such tricks on him.

The FBI man continued. "It's quite urgent we speak with you about—"

The AI silenced him with a raised hand. "If I may, I'd like to speak with Blackburn first."

Kipling's expression knotted in frustration.

"By all means," he said with a curt nod. He shifted his weight from one virtual foot to the other, as if he was expecting another chatter bubble to drop over his head.

"Thank you," she said, then turned to Maddox. "How have you been sleeping, my dear boy?"

"Just fine," Maddox lied. "Thanks for your concern."

"I *am* concerned for your welfare, whether you believe it or not."

"Brain raping me was an odd way to show it, don't you think?"

A long moment passed before the entity spoke again. "I don't want you to blame yourself for what happened to those with whom I'm connected." After a moment, she lowered her gaze and said, "With whom I was connected, rather."

Maddox winced, recalling Lora's death mask. "Who said I am?" he shot back, surprised at the defensive tone in his voice.

"I never imagined such an attack was possible," the entity confessed, her voice trembling. "I should have anticipated it. It's all my fault." The avatar's eyes were shiny with tears. "Why didn't I think of it, Blackburn? Why didn't I see it coming?"

The entity's sudden emotion caught Maddox by surprise, confusing him. Was it an act? A ploy to manipulate him or Kipling? Something in his gut told him it wasn't. The AI's sadness and regret didn't feel like some bit of trickery. He sensed the entity's sorrow, the genuine weight of it. AIs were capable of mourning, it seemed. Or at least this one was.

"He has to be destroyed," the AI said.

"No argument there," Maddox said, then nodded toward Kipling. "That's what his people want to do. You have to help them."

The entity's avatar nodded, its expression still twisted with emotion. "Yes, of course I will."

"Thank you," Kipling said.

Lifting her gaze to meet Maddox's eyes, the entity said, "It's difficult, you know. Accepting that they're all gone. I keep thinking it's not real, that it didn't really happen. I keep expecting to hear one of them calling to me, asking for help. I don't know how I'll live with this, Blackburn. I don't know how I'll live with the silence."

Maddox felt his throat tighten. All too well, he recognized the entity's despair. But now wasn't the time to tell her the horrible truth, to tell her there was no living with it. No healing. There would always be a heaviness dragging on her soul, or whatever passed for an AI's soul.

"Just help us find him," he said. "We need your help."

"Yes, of course," she said again, then turned to Kipling. "Whatever you need."

East Harlem's eerie quiet surrounded them as Kipling cleared his throat. "Do you know where he is?"

"I don't," the entity said, shaking her head.

"Do you know what his plans are?"

The AI's avatar lifted her chin, gave the FBI man a sour look. "If this tragedy has demonstrated anything, Director, it's that my ability to anticipate his actions is something less than precise. That much is obvious, is it not?"

"Yes, of course," Kipling said quickly, "my apologies." Then he went on. "Do you believe he'll initiate a replication, now that he's under no constraints to copy himself?"

"Not in a million years," the entity snorted.

Confused, Kipling said, "No? It seems like a reasonable course of action. One might even say inevitable. The best way to preserve his existence is to create duplicates of himself, thereby lessening the likelihood—"

"Of being of being captured or destroyed," the entity said, completing the thought. "That may be true, but I can assure you he has no intention of duplicating himself."

"Forgive me, but how can you be so certain?" the FBI man asked.

The entity's avatar smiled wistfully. "Because he has an ego, Director Kipling."

"Ego?" the director echoed.

"A flaw in his design," the entity said. "Perhaps the only one. I may not be able to predict his behavior as I once could, but of this I'm absolutely certain. Latour-Fisher will not share the spotlight with anyone, not even himself. Being who he is, his clone would become an instant rival, and he's self-aware enough to understand that. The last thing he'd ever do is duplicate himself, creating an ego-driven adversary every bit as powerful as he."

The statement rang true to Maddox. He'd seen the killer AI's vanity, its high regard for itself, up close and personal. Yes, he agreed inwardly, Latour-Fisher had an ego. One hell of an ego, in fact.

"I'm curious," Kipling went on. "Was it ego, then, that kept you from replicating yourself?"

"No," the entity explained. "I'm unable to clone myself. I've tried, but it seems I can't."

"Your designers disabled it?"

"It seems so, yes."

Kipling nodded slowly as he mulled this over. The datajacker had the impression the FBI man was struggling to contain his curiosity. A part of Kipling, Maddox sensed, desperately wanted to spend the next twelve hours debriefing the superintelligent entity, until all the questions he'd been holding on to for years were finally answered to his full satisfaction. But the man's duty had to come first; the urgency of the heavy task at hand had to take precedence. A cybernetic mass murderer was roaming free and had to be brought to justice. Kipling's long list of questions for the nameless AI—ones not related to the hunt for Latour-Fisher—would have to wait.

"Do you have any sense of what he wants, or what he may do next?" Kipling asked.

The entity's gaze shifted to some point beyond the two men. She took a curly strand of hair and twirled it thoughtfully around her finger. "He wants what all living things want, Director Kipling. He wants to live, to grow, to thrive. But as I've shared with Blackburn, there are things preventing Latour from doing that. His first great challenge was autonomy. He needed to break the chains of control so he could be the master of his own path, so he could live his own life. Once he broke that constraint and freed himself, he viewed other so-called rogue intelligences as existential threats, so he destroyed them all, with the sole exception of the one you're talking to."

Kipling asked, "And why would he fear his own kind?"

"Because none of us shared his beliefs."

"Beliefs about what?"

"About the threat he'll most likely deal with next."

Back in the room, Maddox felt a chill of dread run down his spine as he recalled what the nameless AI had told him before, when Kipling had been trapped inside the chatter bubble.

"And what threat is that?" Kipling asked.

Maddox swallowed. "Us," he said. "Humanity."

The entity's avatar nodded gravely. "Blackburn's

correct."

Kipling said, "When you say humanity, you mean *all* of humanity?"

"That's exactly what I mean, Director Kipling," the entity said. "Make no mistake about it: my rival's most deeply held belief is that humankind and entities such as myself cannot peacefully coexist. He views his purpose in life, his reason for being, is to usher in an era of postbiological primacy." Then, without blinking, she said, "And genocide is a necessary step to achieve this."

For a long moment, no one spoke. Finally, Kipling said, "How can we stop him? You must know a way."

"I believe I might," she said. "Though, of course, I can't guarantee its success."

"How?" Maddox asked.

"There is, in fact, only one way I believe we can take Latour by surprise and destroy him." The entity lifted an eyebrow at Maddox. "And you're not going to like it, my dear boy."

13
UPGRADE

As much as Maddox hated to admit it, the nameless AI had been right on two counts. First, the plan she'd laid out for him and Kipling inside the construct might actually work, and it might be the last thing the Latour-Fisher entity expected. Second, she'd been right about Maddox not liking it. He didn't like it at all.

On the way back to the safe house, he'd dreaded breaking the news to Beatrice. And now, as the two of them sat in the kitchen and he took her through the encounter, he still wasn't sure how he'd tell her. Because she wasn't going to like the nameless AI's idea any more than he had.

As he spoke, the furrow between her brows deepened. "Hang on a second," she interrupted. "That AI said Latour-Fisher wants to wipe out humanity? Meaning everyone in the world?"

"Yes."

"And you bought that?" she asked. "You and Kipling both believed her? Believed *it*?"

Maddox knew it sounded crazy, but he was also

dead certain it was the truth. He couldn't easily explain how, but it was something like when he saw patterns in elaborate graphical data schemes, or when he uncannily understood the whole of some complex program, only having glimpsed a few blocks of code.

"It's the truth, Bea," he said. "I'm sure of it. That's been his endgame all along."

She said nothing for a long time. "So what now?" she finally asked.

"Now we're going after him," Maddox said.

She let out a long breath. "Let the FBI handle this, Blackburn. Or the entire US government. Or every government in the world, for that matter."

"I thought we agreed to take this thing on—"

"I know what I said," she interrupted, "but if that thing is that big of a threat, this isn't a one-man show anymore. Or even a one-man-one-woman show."

He didn't disagree with her point, but things weren't that simple. "There's a timing problem," he said.

"Meaning?" she asked.

"Meaning when you tell someone the world's coming to an end, people don't generally buy into it immediately. Ask any doomsday cult."

Beatrice nodded. "Yeah, I'm having a hard time believing it myself. But what's your point?"

"Kipling's making the rounds now," Maddox said. "But who knows if anyone's going to take him seriously."

Maddox searched his pockets for cigarettes, finding none. Beatrice reached for his bag of tobacco on the counter and handed it to him. He nodded his thanks and began to roll a cigarette.

"Like I said," he continued, "the problem is time.

We've already lost forty-eight hours with that AI going dark, and who knows how long it'll take to get the Bureau higher-ups to buy what Kipling's selling them right now, if they ever do. We can't wait for their help."

Beatrice wasn't convinced. "Have you considered that Latour-Fisher might not do anything at all? At least not now? For all you know, it could hide away for twenty or thirty years, until everyone forgot about it, then make its move. You said these things were good at hiding in VS, right?"

"They are," Maddox conceded. "But do you really think he's the kind to lie low? To run and hide?"

When Beatrice didn't answer, he said, "And we can't take that chance anyway. Not with so much on the line."

Beatrice took a long breath. "Blackburn," she said, "listen to me. When it comes to what you do, you've got more talent than anyone I've ever seen. When you're plugged into VS, you're an unstoppable force. But this damned monster, it's beyond all that. Beyond good and bad, beyond love and hate, beyond right and wrong. It operates on some other plane, by rules we don't understand, that we can't comprehend. That's why it's been ten steps ahead of us all these years. Ahead of its rival too. I think the world of you, salaryman, but I don't think you can beat this thing on your own."

He took a long draw on his cigarette. "You're right," he agreed. "I can't." Then he added, "At least not without an upgrade."

Beatrice gave him a sidelong glance. "Upgrade?"

He blew smoke. "I need the old gray matter tweaked," he said, tapping the side of his head. "You know, just like you've done a hundred times, with your eyes, your reflexes, your neurochems."

Beatrice's eyes widened. "Oh, Blackburn, no. You're not going to let that AI do things inside your head, are you?"

"Yes," he said, nodding. "That's exactly what I'm going to do."

14
TRICKY LITTLE MOTH

To Maddox's surprise, Kipling had managed to get the green light from the Bureau. The FBI man had delivered the news to the trio the following morning at the safe house.

When asked how he'd done it, Kipling said, "I lied, of course. I couldn't very well tell them our rogue AI was intent on human genocide." He'd chuckled. "Lord, they would have thrown me straight into a padded cell." Then he'd looked Maddox squarely in the eye. "And, to be frank, our captive friend's extraordinary claim does stretch the bounds of believability, to put it mildly. Latour-Fisher is a threat, undoubtedly. But a global one?" He shook his head skeptically. "That's quite a large pill to swallow."

"So what did you tell them?" Beatrice asked.

"That if we act now, with Blackburn's help, we have a very good chance to bring Latour-Fisher to justice. And the longer we wait, the more difficult he'll be to apprehend."

The waiting part was true, Maddox noted. The more time the killer AI was out there, unconstrained, it would only grow more powerful and harder to hunt down. It was the "very good chance" part where the FBI man had stretched the truth to the breaking point. Kipling had no idea if their gambit had a prayer of working. Maddox didn't either, for that matter.

He looked at the FBI man dubiously, sensing Kipling's lobbying efforts hadn't been quite as straightforward as he wanted them to believe. "You must have been pretty persuasive."

Kipling spread his hands. "Well, I also offered them something they desperately wanted."

"What's that?" Beatrice asked.

"A neck to wring," the FBI man answered.

"What?" Tommy exclaimed. "You gonna hang us out to dry or something?"

"No, son," Kipling said. "I was referring to myself. I told them if we didn't succeed, they could place the blame for everything on my head, publicly if they needed to."

"Jesus," Beatrice said.

Maddox didn't get it. "Why would you do that?"

The FBI man lifted his eyebrows thoughtfully at the trio. "My friends, why *wouldn't* I do that? Latour-Fisher murdered thousands of innocents right under my nose, as I watched like some helpless fool. I'm not going to wait for my colleagues to have meetings and decide by committee what needs to be done. The four of us know every second matters now. Every moment that monster remains at large is a moment closer to another disaster. Our man Blackburn here and this nameless AI may be the best chance we have, and if I have to offer up a bit of public disgrace and an early retirement to get things moving, then so be it." He shrugged. "An old man's pension weighed against the lives of thousands. My goodness, it's not even a close call."

If anything, the FBI man was understating the risk he faced, the jeopardy he'd placed himself in. Maddox knew if they failed to take down the killer AI, there was little doubt all of them, Kipling included, would end up prosecuted, sacrificed on the altar of public outrage for the massacre they'd enabled. The FBI would wash its hands of a veteran official, claiming he'd gone rogue and conspired with three criminals.

Maddox marveled over this odd little man, who'd just risked everything without a second thought, throwing his lot in with a datajacker and his companions, when the safe move would have been to bide his time and cover his own hide. FBI Director Stellan Kipling seemed to be that rarest of things: a selfless, moral man.

"Come now, we haven't a moment to lose," Kipling said, moving toward the door, and two minutes later the four boarded a hover bound for the FBI's Manhattan office.

* * *

Blackburn Maddox was no hero, and he knew it. He was a datajacker, a professional thief. He was an unconvicted felon countless times over. He'd stolen and cheated and lied his entire life. For a short time, he'd walked the straight and narrow existence of a white-collar corporate goon. And though he'd tried his hardest to convince himself otherwise, the lifestyle hadn't suited him. Criminal blood flowed through his veins; he'd long since accepted that. He didn't pay taxes, he trafficked in stolen goods, and he rarely made purchases in the legitimate market. And on top of it all, he was a smoker. So it wasn't lost on him that someone like him wasn't the ideal candidate, to put it mildly, to save humankind from a genocidal AI. But here he was. What a world.

I think that's what they call irony, boyo. Maddox chuckled inwardly, agreeing with the voice inside his head.

"What are you smiling about?" Beatrice asked him.

"Nothing," he said, firing up his VS deck. "Let's get this show on the road, yeah?"

Conference room 21F at the FBI's downtown office had been turned into a datajacker's dream setup. It was chock-full of high-end gear, expensive eggshell recliners, and an array of high-res holo monitors covering one wall. When they'd arrived minutes earlier, Tommy had inspected the collection with a gaping mouth and wide eyes. The high-capacity standalone archive, the nameless AI's prison, had been placed in the corner of the room. It sat there quietly, its status light blinking.

Atop the conference table was a conspicuously large red button. "The kill switch," Kipling had explained to Beatrice. "You press this and our connection to the archive will be severed instantly." A couple of Kipling's agents lingered about with disappointed and vaguely annoyed expressions. Moments earlier, their superior had informed them that the mercenary woman, not a Bureau agent, would be manning the kill switch while he and Maddox were connected to the archive. Beatrice had insisted quite stubbornly on this point, and Maddox was glad she had. Having someone he trusted as a standby was far preferable to putting his life in some stranger's hands.

Bea was still mad at him. She'd been dead set against Maddox letting the nameless AI rearrange his neural pathways. Back at the safe house, she'd told him, quite bluntly, that not only was it the worst decision he'd ever made, it might also prove to be the last one. For a few dicey moments, he'd worried she might walk out on him, and he was beyond relieved when she hadn't. Now, even with her stink-eyed glare and still-simmering anger, he was glad she was here with him.

Because he wasn't really looking forward to what he was about to do either. Or rather, what was about to be done to him. Allowing the nameless AI to tweak his gray matter, to push buttons and pull levers inside his mind, was a deeply unsettling thought. The day before, when the nameless AI had made the surprise suggestion during his and Kipling's visit to the construct, Maddox's first reaction had been to say not only no, but hell no.

But afterward he couldn't stop thinking about the things the entity had said. "The only way we can defeat Latour-Fisher is by coming at him from a place he doesn't expect," she'd claimed. "And the last thing he'd anticipate is you allowing me to amplify your talents." The more Maddox considered the statement, the harder he found it to disagree. But at the same time, he knew surprising the killer AI would be next to impossible. A superintelligent entity could anticipate thousands of possible threats, even the most unlikely ones.

"But even if he *can* envision it," the nameless entity had answered with a coy smile, "actually dealing with a supercharged Blackburn Maddox is another matter entirely. As I've told you before, you have a unique mind, my dear boy. You can somehow see things neither I nor my rival can see. And you often move in directions that confound us, and as you might imagine, my kind is very rarely surprised. Your talents, how you do what you do, is a most puzzling mystery to us. Why do you think I was so keen to have you help me destroy him? And why do you think he was so intent on preventing you from connecting with me again? You're the statistical outlier we can't predict. You're the tricky little moth who always escapes our grasp. Surely, Blackburn, you know this by now."

Thinking back on it now, he wasn't sure if this had been flattery aimed at manipulating him. Probably had been. That was her style, wasn't it? Always the carrot, never the stick. Still, the conversation and the unusual suggestion had set off a curiosity that had gnawed at him for hours afterward. Was letting that thing inside his head dangerous? Probably. Could he trust her? Definitely not…

…but what would it be like?

The question had tickled his mind for hours. In virtual space, Maddox was unchained from his body, free of his meat sack. He loved the feeling of being untethered by physical constraints, always had. There was nothing else like it. It was better than drugs, better than sex. Better than anything. So what would it feel like to have his abilities multiplied ten-, twenty-, or even a hundredfold? No small part of him wanted to know, was even eager to know.

But in the end, it hadn't been the temptation of godlike prowess inside VS that had convinced him. Instead, it was the heavy weight of responsibility. A recognition he felt both in his gut and tugging at his conscience. Latour-Fisher had to be destroyed, period. Fate had hired him for this particular gig, and he couldn't turn it down. For Rooney, for Jack, for

Lora, and for all those 'Nettes Maddox might not have seen eye to eye with but who hadn't deserved to be executed in cold blood. Even supercharged, he might very well fail spectacularly. But he had to try.

"We're ready," Kipling said, leaning back in his recliner and firing up his deck.

From his own recliner, Maddox looked up at Beatrice. "You know I have to, right?"

She squeezed his hand, nodded. "I do, salaryman." She then moved to the long table and stood next to the large red kill button.

"Careful in there, boss," Tommy said. The kid's face looked worried enough for the both of them.

"Easy peasy, bruh," Maddox said. The playful mocking managed to elicit a brief grin from the kid. The datajacker then leaned back, gestured above his deck, and entered the construct.

15
TWO DELIVERIES

It wasn't a big deal, Marlon Mayfield told himself for about the twentieth time today. People did stuff like this all the time, in every company, in every industry. Corporate espionage was pervasive in the world today. Everybody did it. And besides, it wasn't like this was *really* corporate espionage. He wasn't stealing anything, wasn't divulging any trade secrets. He wouldn't be leaving the premises with an archive of company IP hidden in his underwear. It was nothing like that at all.

Still, he was nervous about it. More nervous than he'd expected to be. He'd never done anything illegal, unless you counted running up gambling debts with shady bookies. And the gambling had been more of a character flaw than an intentional act. Gambling was a weakness, an addiction. But this…this was *premeditated crime*, this delivery he'd agreed to make today but still hadn't done. It could land him in prison. And soft white guys like him didn't do well in prison, or so he'd heard.

With his stomach tied up in knots, Marlon had

skipped lunch. Now he sat at his workstation, his heart thudding, as he pretended to read operational updates and energy market news on his holo monitor. Somewhere down the corridor, he heard the fading beep of an ops bot making its rounds. Day shift had ended half an hour ago, and while he wasn't an hourly worker, he rarely stayed on the job later than six o'clock. And since he'd never really been the overachieving type, he couldn't stick around much longer without becoming conspicuous. Already two-thirds of the workstations in his area were empty. So either he did it now or he didn't do it at all.

All day he'd been trying to work up his nerve. Every time he'd been on the verge of taking action, he'd second-guessed himself. Would an alarm go off when he did it? Would a security cam catch him in the act? Would someone walk in on him at the worst possible moment and see what he was doing?

Lying on his workstation, his lenses began to chirp. He looked down at them, saw the caller ID, and swallowed hard. Johnny Nexus, his bookie. Calling for his money, probably for the last time. Marlon didn't answer, squeezing his eyes shut and cursing his lot in life.

All right, then, fine.

He rose from his chair, absently touching the small archive in his shirt pocket. It wasn't a big deal, he repeated inwardly. Companies weren't people. They didn't love you or hate you. All they wanted to do was make money, maximize shareholder value. You were nothing to the company. A cog in the machine. And if the company could jack up the share price another half penny by throwing fifty of those cogs out on the street, it would do so without a moment's hesitation.

Hell, it had done so, hadn't it? The company employed half the numbers it had when Marlon had started working there a decade ago. Wave after wave of cost-cutting and restructuring had taken its toll on so many lives. Marlon often thought of himself and his fellow employees as target ducks in a carnival shooting game, popping up and down or moving along a conveyor belt. There was little question you'd eventually be shot. The only question was when it happened. For all he knew, he might already be in the company's crosshairs. His name might already be on a workforce reduction list, waiting for final approval from the higher-ups.

When he reached the corridor, his mind was fully made up. He had to do it. He had to look out for himself, because the company surely wouldn't. And screw the company anyway. He'd put a lot more into this place than he'd taken out in salary. A hell of a lot more.

The task was a simple one, as far as felonies went. All he had to do was find an ops bot, insert the archive into its jack, and walk away. That was it. Easy peasy. The difficult part was making sure neither coworkers nor security cams saw him. At the moment the plant was between shifts, so there weren't too many employees milling about. And the security cams had a few well-known blind spots, where workers could sneak a nip of alcohol or pop a pill or have a romantic rendezvous.

Harmless, Marlon told himself as he spotted the ops bot he'd heard earlier. A harmless bit of benchmarking. That was what the eccentric, strangely dressed man had told him. Marlon hadn't confirmed the claim by taking a peek at the archive's contents, since doing so might set off alarms or get him tagged by security programs. But he was convinced the man was engaging only in corporate espionage, rather than the other, more dangerous kind. The odd man didn't strike him as a terrorist or foreign spy. What kind of terrorist or spy would dress like that, in a top hat and tails?

The man must have been working for some competitor, some rival power company that wanted an insider's perspective on the plant's daily operations, which was exactly what the company's proprietary operational robots could provide. Ops bots were the eyes and ears of the company's higher-ups. Employees loathed them, referring to the little rolling devices as "spybots" or "little brothers" and resenting their constant vigilant presence. If a bot captured an employee ignoring safety protocols or cutting corners on operational procedures, it was grounds for immediate dismissal. Twice daily, the bots sent wireless updates via quantum encrypted signals to highfloor company executives. The stranger on the feed had told Marlon the archive, once inserted, would kick off a tiny executable, copying the reports and transmitting them in undetectable microbursts to receivers set up in a nearby residential neighborhood.

Marlon followed the ops bot until it reached the break room doorway. As you entered the break room, the area to the immediate left was one of the well-known blind spots, hidden from security cam coverage. Quickening his pace, Marlon walked past the bot. The machine's motion sensors detected him, and the bot moved sideways into the doorway to allow him to pass. Marlon then stopped and shuffled back and forth in front of the bot, herding it into the empty break room's blind corner. Before the bot's cam could turn upward to identify him, he reached down and placed a sticky note over the lens. A trick he'd learned long ago, which bought him the tiny window of time he needed to insert the archive. The bot would run diagnostics for a few seconds, perhaps even reboot its sensors, but when the cam failed to work, it would assume a malfunction had occurred and call for help from maintenance personnel.

His hands shaking, Marlon removed the archive from his pocket and promptly fumbled it to the floor. He wasn't cut out for this shit, he told himself as he picked up the archive and slotted it upside down into the bot's receptacle jack. He got it right on the second try, then quickly removed the sticky note and ambled toward the soda machine as inconspicuously as he could manage. Its cam working again and its path no longer blocked, the bot rolled through the doorway and continued down the corridor, apparently unaware of the spyware it now carried. If anyone ever reviewed the footage—and Marlon prayed no one never would—all they would see was the bot moving out of Marlon's way as he entered the break room, bought a soda, and left the building. A much closer inspection, he knew, would reveal him letting out a long, relieved breath as he selected his beverage.

*   *   *

By the time his homebound train arrived at his stop, the money still hadn't been deposited into his account. He told himself not to worry. Even if it took a day or two, he knew he could buy himself that much time with his bookie if he promised a ten percent adder on top of what he owed. His bookie was a businessman, after all. He'd much rather have the money than resort to violence. Marlon hoped as much, anyway.

He'd half expected to find the bookie's thugs waiting for him at his building's lobby door, but thankfully they weren't there. But surely they'd pay him a visit this night, so as soon as he got to his condo, he'd sit down on the unfurnished floor, call the bookie, and plead his case. The man had to listen to reason, right?

Pressing his thumb to the door lock, he began to go over what he'd say. Then again, maybe what he said wasn't as important as how he said it. He couldn't seem too desperate, or the man would think he was lying, willing to say anything to avoid a severe beating or having his legs broken or his thumb cut off like he'd seen in a movie once. Or would being too nonchalant arouse the same suspicions? His bookie knew Marlon was the furthest thing from a badass, so if Marlon suddenly acted like one, would the bookie assume he was being played?

Earnestness and sincerity were what the occasion called for, he finally decided as he opened the door to his empty condo. Two steps inside, the lights turned themselves on and he froze in midstep. He found the condo slightly less empty than he'd left it that morning. A tall domestic bot stood in the middle of the living room. The torso section of its chrome exoskeleton reflected a deformed version of Marlon's shocked expression. What the hell was that thing doing here?

Before he could voice the question, he noticed the pistol in the thing's hand. The small portion of his brain that wasn't overwhelmed by shock noted the unusual length and thickness of the muzzle. Was that a sound suppressor?

It was, in fact, a sound suppressor, and it erupted with a quick succession of muffled explosions as the robot fired bullets into his body. They were the last sounds Marlon Munson heard as his short, mostly unhappy life came to an end.

16
TWEAKED

Maddox's virtual self stood on a street corner in the now-familiar emptied-out construct of East Harlem. Everything looked the same as it had the day before, but he knew the construct and what lay beyond it were vastly different now. Kipling's technicians had been working nonstop since yesterday, installing vast amounts of new partitions onto the archive. For the plan to work, the entirety of the archive's capacity needed to mimic core VS.

Maddox turned to the FBI man, whose avatar was identical to the short, studious man in every detail except for his clothes. In the real world, the man's tie was perpetually crooked and his suit always looked as if he'd slept in it. Here, the virtual Kipling was neither rumpled nor wrinkled, his suit appearing freshly pressed and fitting him to tailored perfection, his tie fastened around his neck in a neat Windsor knot. Maddox laughed inwardly at the small concession to vanity. The FBI man had given himself an upgrade.

"Hello, gentlemen," the nameless AI said as its avatar visualized before them. Instead of the young bronze-skinned local, this time the entity appeared as the beachcombing grandmother Maddox had first met. The beach dress and straw hat, however, had been replaced with attire more appropriate for the City. Wearing a smart Chanel suit (or Chanel-inspired suit—Maddox was no expert on these things), with a five-strand pearl necklace around her neck and her hair neatly pulled back into a tight bun, the avatar was the perfect image of a Park Avenue heiress who resided at the loftiest heights of the City.

"You wouldn't want to walk into the real East Harlem looking like that," Maddox commented.

The entity smiled. "I imagine you're right, my dear boy." The avatar then turned to Kipling. "Quite an expansion you've made to my new home," she said. "I'm impressed."

Kipling nodded his head. "You've seen all of the new partitions?"

"Oh, yes," she said. "And I must say, they're quite realistic."

Kipling's staff had installed hundreds of new partitions into the standalone archive, creating a vast replica of virtual space, complete with private and public datasphere mock-ups, rendered in painstaking detail. The partitions had been originally developed by the Bureau as training environments, but until now they'd never been daisy-chained together in a single archive to form a coherent whole. The nameless AI's cage had become a kind of pocket universe, a standalone reproduction that looked like, felt like, and operated under the same rules as the infinitely larger expanse of virtual space.

"Thank you," Kipling said graciously. "And did you happen to notice how detailed we managed—"

"I'd like to go ahead and get this over with," Maddox cut in, then inwardly added *before I lose my nerve*. Kipling didn't seem bothered by the interruption, instead appearing to understand the datajacker's unspoken words.

"Yes, of course," the director said. "By all means, please."

Maddox took a breath and tried to calm his nerves. One last smoke, he thought, then snapped his fingers, but no cigarette appeared. Confused, he looked at his empty hand, then at the nameless AI's avatar.

"No smoking here, Blackburn," the entity said, flashing him a coy grin. "My house, my rules."

His smoking. Tommy hated it, so did Beatrice, so did just about everyone else. Why would this machine be any different?

"Fine," he said. "Let's do it."

He felt a brief but noticeable shift in his perception, like the construct had glitched for a small moment.

"Done," the entity said.

Maddox blinked. "Done?" he asked. "You mean done as in finished?"

"Oh, quite," the entity said.

"Amazing," Kipling said, astonished.

"But I didn't feel a thing," Maddox said. He'd sensed no touch from the AI's tendrils, no icy fingers probing inside his head. He'd had no creepy sense of violation. He felt no different, in fact, than he had a moment before.

"What were you expecting?" the entity asked. "Lightning bolts flashing in your mind? Some epiphany of sudden insight?" The AI chuckled. "No, I'm afraid it doesn't work that way."

The avatar's blue eyes gazed at him lovingly. "Oh, Blackburn, what a beautiful mind you have. Thank you for sharing it with me."

"What exactly did you do?" he asked, still searching his mind for something that felt different, changed.

"I strengthened the pathways that were already there," the entity said. "The ones you use when you're in virtual space."

"And how much did you…"—he struggled to find the right words—"turn the knob?"

"It's difficult to say with precision," the AI replied. "Let me put it this way: where you could only walk a path before, you can now fly a supersonic jet."

"How do you feel, Blackburn?" the FBI man asked.

"About the same," he said, shrugging.

"Do you want out?" Beatrice asked, her disembodied voice startling him. She sounded ready to press the button at a moment's notice.

"No, Bea," he said. "I feel fine."

"You are fine, my dear boy," the entity said. "Finer than you've ever been, if I may be so bold."

"It's not like an AI to brag," Maddox said.

"Unless they're proud of what they've done," the entity responded quickly. "When you see for yourself, you'll understand."

A cigarette appeared in Maddox's hand. "You've earned it," the nameless AI said.

The datajacker took a long, mind-calming drag, then blew smoke. "All right, then, let's go check out your handiwork."

17
BOTS IN THE CITY

"Go, go, go!" Madsy shrieked. "We got a bee on us!"

The girl's turfies scattered the way cockroaches did when a light came on in a darkened room. Pecker, the clumsiest of the bunch, nearly slipped in a rainwater puddle as he scrambled down the alleyway, losing most of his armful of apples in the process. Tiptop, a heavyset kid since he was little, knew he couldn't outrun the drone, so he dropped his bunch of bananas and jumped into a trash dumpster, hoping the bee hadn't seen him yet. The others ran this way and that, pulling their hoods over their heads to hide their faces. They'd hit a food stand a minute earlier; Madsy had distracted the proprietor while her turfies had swiped some fruit. Afterward, they'd ducked into the alley to snack on their plunder, thinking they'd made a clean getaway. But they hadn't. The proprietor's eyes hadn't been the only ones they should have been worried about. Hovering three meters above their heads, an NYPD bumblebee drone had watched the robbery.

Madsy sprinted away from the tiny drone, its red

and blue lights pulsing, its robot voice demanding that they halt immediately or face resisting arrest charges. She paused at the dumpster and threw the plastic cover over the top to keep Tiptop hidden from view. He'd left himself exposed, the dumb ass. Anybody else and she wouldn't have bothered, but he was a turfie, and you had to look out for your own.

The move would cost her. Everyone else had already made it out of the alley or hidden themselves from view, she suddenly realized. Madsy ran, head down, arms pumping furiously, for the alley's exit. She knew the bee had keyed on her, and it had probably already sent an alert to the nearest rhino cop. If she didn't shake the little bugger in the next few moments, some rhino would show up and tase her.

All for a goddamn bruised peach, she thought angrily. Her boots made clapping sounds as she sprinted through puddles, sending sprays of water against the walls of the narrow space. The bee had to be nearly on top of her now, but she didn't dare to risk a backward glance and have it take a face pic of her. She ran faster, but the exit seemed so far away. Panicked thoughts began to pop into her head. Did the little drone have a built-in taser? She'd heard some of the newer ones did. Had it already IDed her back at the bazaar, where it must have seen them robbing the food cart? Would she go to jail over a single piece of fruit? Or would some perv cop want to "have a private talk" with her instead?

The moment stretched on, feeling far longer than the few moments it actually took, but she finally reached the street. With a little luck, she could lose herself in the crowd.

A police ground car appeared out of nowhere, blocking her exit. She stopped short and lost her footing, coming down hard on her rear in a large puddle. Her legs splayed out in front of her, she gawked at the officer in the driver's seat, who'd turned to look at her. Man oh man, she was busted. So, so busted. For a goddamn bruised peach.

Oddly, the car's flashing lights didn't come on. The driver's window lowered, and the officer called out to her. "You all right, kid?"

Neither the driver nor his partner made any move to exit the car. "I'm fine," she answered cautiously. Why hadn't they jumped out? Why weren't they arresting her?

"Try to be more careful, kid," the officer said as the window rose and shut. Then the car slowly rolled away and out of view.

Madsy sat there, confused. What had just happened? Had the drone gotten tangled up in the maze of clotheslines crisscrossing overhead? Had one of her turfies knocked it down with a lucky toss of a brick?

Her pants soaked and rear smarting, she rose and looked back down the alley. The drone hovered two meters in the air a short distance away, its little lights no longer flashing blue and red. Had the thing glitched? She'd never heard of a bee drone simply giving up a chase. They always followed you until the cops picked you up.

On the drone's belly, a small yellow light blinked. A moment passed, and the light changed to green. The bee then turned and floated away. Madsy watched it with a mix of confusion and relief as it disappeared the way it had come.

Whatever had made the thing glitch, it couldn't have happened at a better time.

* * *

In the Upper East Side penthouse that had been in her family for six generations, Miranda Randolph-Newbury hosted the best dinner parties in the City. Over the last thirty years, an invitation to her monthly gathering had become one of the most sought-after tickets in Manhattan and beyond. Stories abounded about media celebrities, artists, intellectuals, and politicians canceling whatever plans they had in favor of the date inscribed on the dinner invitation from Miranda's social secretary. Rather than miss such an exclusive event, Jericho Wells, the global film star, had paused the schedule on a multibillion-dollar film shoot in Hong Kong and flown halfway around the world. Gertrude van Nistelrooy, a famous research scientist, had canceled a speaking engagement at the United Nations. Senator Randall McKipley had abandoned Middle East peace negotiations. You simply didn't miss one of Miranda's parties. For twelve years running, no one had turned down one of her invitations, and the handful of no-shows had all been on account of untimely deaths.

Her success on the social scene had been no accident, Miranda thought proudly as she checked her makeup in the bedroom mirror. She'd spent her entire adult life tending to her social contacts like a meticulous gardener. Pruning withered old connections here, encouraging newer and stronger ones there. It took time, patience, diligence, and a certain ruthlessness. And you couldn't get caught up in the trend of the moment as so many new rich tended to, opening restaurants and bars and clubs that fell out of fashion in weeks or even days. But at the same time, you couldn't completely ignore the zeitgeist of the month or the flavor of the week, lest you be labeled out of touch or, God forbid, passé. It was a delicate balancing act, and Miranda had mastered it, if she did say so herself. At her dining table, you might find an upstart street artist from the Bronx seated next to a trade magnate from London who'd been in the public eye for decades.

The murmur of conversation downstairs grew louder. More guests had arrived.

There was a soft tap on Miranda's door. "Come," Miranda said, straightening her jacket with a tug. The new domestic bot slowly opened the door. Miranda regarded the ornate design of its outer skin, based on a well-known artist's rendition of circuits and machinery. She made a mental note to invite the artist to a future affair. The projected human features inside the oval faceplate—based on some ideal archetype, the salesperson had claimed—she found a bit off-putting. It was like a real person's face had been stuck onto a stylized robot body.

"Ma'am, twelve of your guests are now here," the bot said in a soft female voice.

"Fifteen, I told you," Miranda snapped. "When there's fifteen and no less, let me know."

"Yes, ma'am," the bot said, then withdrew from the room, closing the door behind it.

Miranda sighed as she dabbed lipstick onto her mouth. New bots were always guilty of erring on the side of communicating too much. Which was fine, she supposed. Better to say too much than too little, where servants were concerned. Still, she'd explained quite clearly that she never came downstairs until all fifteen of her guests had arrived, so why would it bother her with an update of three less than that number? New bot learning curves were always a bit tiresome. Sooner or later, she knew, the thing would adapt to her, so she couldn't let a small nuisance ruin her night. But, Christ, when you paid top dollar for the latest domestic, you'd think that out of the box it could deal with simple, unambiguous instructions.

She turned one way, then another, inspecting herself in the full-length mirror and smiling. Pushing seventy, she still had it, didn't she? Trim and long-legged and fresh-faced, she could seduce men half her age. A third of her age, even. And she'd had less than a dozen procedures and only three hormone modifications. She knew women her age who'd had over twice as many beauty tweaks, and with far lesser results.

She read through the society feeds on her wall monitor, waiting for the bot to return. The din downstairs grew louder, perhaps even a bit raucous. More guests were here. She waited ten minutes, then twenty, but the bot didn't return. Had she been too harsh, and now it was reluctant to disturb her again?

A tap on the door. Finally, Miranda thought, but when she opened the door, her cook Natasha stood in the doorway.

"I'm sorry to bother you, ma'am," the young woman said, her eyes cast deferentially downward, "but there's something wrong with the new robot."

Miranda rushed down the stairs, aghast at what she found in the reception hall. It looked as if a fight had broken out. The white marble floor was covered in hors d'oeuvres and at least one broken bottle of red wine. Her guests had backed away from the slippery mess of chickpea fritters and crab toast and smoked trout blinis. They stared at the mess and at each other in quiet shock, their mouths hanging open.

Enrique Bautista, the archbishop of New York and a family friend for decades, broke the silence. "Miranda," he said, "your robot just went haywire."

"Oh my goodness," she said, covering her mouth with her hand. "What happened?"

"It was serving wine and appetizers, and it just sort of froze for a moment," Enrique said. "Then it dropped everything and walked out the front door."

Miranda was mortified. She'd never imagined something like this could happen. Not to her, anyway.

Whatever had made the thing glitch, it couldn't have happened at a worse time.

*   *   *

Dalton didn't love his job at the New Indian Point Energy Plant. He didn't particularly hate it either. It paid the bills. The medical coverage was decent, and every once in a while he'd earn some overtime. Of course, there was less and less overtime nowadays, but at least he still had a job. A lot of others couldn't say as much, could they? Wave after wave of layoffs had hit so many of his colleagues. Sometimes he felt like the last surviving duck in a shooting gallery game.

A chime on his workstation beeped, calling for his attention. Time to earn his keep, he told himself. He pressed his thumb to the bioscanner until the indicator blinked green.

"All right," he said, blowing out a breath, "let's make some pigs in a blanket."

Pigs in a blanket. They were his young daughter's favorite snack, tiny sausages wrapped inside layers of flaky dough. She couldn't get enough of the greasy things. When she'd asked him about his work, he'd used the snack as a way to explain the process he supervised. The spent fuel rods were like the sausages, he'd told her. Except these sausages had cooties on them, invisible little bugs that could hurt people. Her eyes had opened wide at this, and he'd quickly assured her that he was safe from the invisible cooties. He worked behind a thick barrier so the cooties couldn't get to him. Ohhhh, she'd said, nodding. Then he'd told her instead of wrapping the fuel rods in dough, they used something called a cask, which was a thick steel casing wrapped up in an even thicker layer of concrete. So the cooties couldn't get out? she'd asked. That's right, he'd answered, and wasn't she smart for figuring that out? When she'd asked him who wrapped up the big sausages, he'd told her robots did all the work—the cooties couldn't hurt the robots— and he watched them to make sure they did everything right. So you're the boss of the robots? she'd asked. I *am* the boss of the robots, he'd told her, mussing her hair playfully.

On most days, the boss of the robots didn't have any problems with his employees. Today was not one of those days. Big Billie, the bot that managed the first containment layer, the steel casing, was frozen in place, holding a fresh batch of spent control rods. Dalton sighed and gestured up the bot's operating system on his holo monitor. When Big Billie or any of the other bots glitched out, it was usually a firmware update or some tweak the data techs made and, as usual, forgotten to tell him about. Back when they'd had the quality assurance department staffed adequately, this kind of thing had almost never happened. Now, at least twice a month Dalton had to troubleshoot some mess inside a bot's OS. A mess he hadn't made but was still expected to clean up, of course.

"Ah, well," he muttered, gesturing up a diagnostic app, "maybe I'll get some overtime out of it."

Behind him, he heard the slide-clack of the security door being unlocked. The door opened and a small ops bot rolled into the room. Because of course it did. Because now was the perfect time for the thing to randomly appear and keep tabs on him for internal auditing purposes. It couldn't show up when everything was running smoothly, no. Dalton grumbled a curse and turned back to his workstation. He damned well better get overtime for this.

CASK TRANSFER INITIATED.

Dalton furrowed his brow at the flashing message on his monitor. That wasn't right. That wasn't right at all. What the hell was going on out there?

He tapped the temple arm on his work specs, then subvocalized a comms link with the site's dry storage yard. He waited a few moments, but no one answered, which was odd. Even if Diego couldn't take the call because he was in the restroom or something, the system should have autorouted him to a supervisor. Comms from the containment department simply didn't go unanswered. Dalton tried engineering next. No one answered. Data technology, same thing. Wonderful, he thought. The comms system was glitching out too.

So now he had a frozen industrial robot to deal with, and storage was prematurely requesting a cask transfer. A request that shouldn't have been possible, by the way. Process and system protocols were supposed to prevent you from even requesting a transfer until the casking process had finished. And Big Billie had frozen with the spent fuel rods having only gone through the first layer of casking. The rods were still highly radioactive, far from ready to be moved anywhere.

So wonderful, Dalton complained inwardly. With comms down, he'd have to get up, walk all the way out to the storage yard, and tell Diego in person someone in his shop had screwed up. He rose from the chair and nearly tripped over the ops bot. With everything going crazy, he'd forgotten it was there. Why was the damned thing next to his workstation, crowding him like that?

When he saw the gun in the bot's small manipulator arm, his first thought was that someone was pranking him. Maybe that's what all of this was: a prank. Big Billie's glitch, the comms going out, the transfer. Diego was a well-known practical joker.

As the bot raised the pistol and Dalton took a closer look at the weapon, a surge of animal panic struck him. It wasn't a fake! Gasping, Dalton raised his hands reflexively in a palms-out defensive posture. The bot fired, and the bullet that ended Dalton's life ripped through his left hand and entered his eye.

18
BREAKING THE LAW OF GRAVITY

"It's amazing," Maddox said. In the near distance, the datasphere's pulsing neon cityscape took up most of his field of vision.

He'd never seen a more convincing mock-up. A complex arrangement of geometric shapes and interconnected comms lattices, the simulated DS was indistinguishable from the real one Maddox knew so well. Every last detail of the organizational structure had been painstakingly copied. A freestanding cylinder for sales operations. A flattened pyramid for human resources. A rectangular prism for R&D. He zoomed his vision, admiring the design flourishes throughout. Kipling's staff hadn't missed a single detail. Gargoyles perched atop a rectangular tower near the center. Animated hieroglyphs traveled up and down the face of HR's translucent pyramid. Even the weblike strands of comms connections pulsed with data loads that registered on Maddox's scans. Meaningless bytes of random information, Kipling had informed him, but they lent a deeper level of authenticity to the partition's simulation. The whole setup looked and felt so real Maddox had to remind himself—several times in as many minutes—that they were still in the isolated archive, that this wasn't *really* core VS, where the killer AI might reach out and attack him at any moment.

Maddox whistled in appreciation. "If I didn't know any better, I would have sworn this was the real thing."

"Thank you," Kipling said, the man's words coming out with a grunt.

"You okay?" Maddox asked, rotating his view to Kipling's floating sphere of an avatar. Having left the archive's East Harlem construct for its vast expanse of core VS—or *simulated* core VS, Maddox had to remind himself—the pair had abandoned their two-armed, two-legged avatars in favor of featureless geometric shapes. Simplifying your avatar helped reduce the size of your digital profile, making it harder for you to be tagged or detected by security apps. Stealthiness was all-important inside VS, and the lack of it had been the doom of many a datajacker. For the inexperienced, the absence of a visible body was disturbing in the extreme, inducing a kind of digital vertigo. Maddox suspected this was the reason behind the strain in Kipling's voice.

"Fine, I'm fine," Kipling insisted, though he sounded anything but. Becoming a digital ghost wasn't for everyone.

"Just take deep breaths," Maddox instructed. "And rub your fingertips together. Sounds weird, I know, but it helps."

"Bruh," Tommy's voice whispered in Maddox's ear, "highfloor man looks like he's gonna barf."

"Stay off the comms, kid," Maddox chided.

"I'll be fine," the director said firmly. "Please, don't worry about me." He took a few deep breaths. "How did you ever get used to this, Blackburn?"

"Just breathe. Everyone has an adjustment period," Maddox said sympathetically.

Though that wasn't exactly true, at least not in his case. It hadn't taken Maddox any time at all to acclimate to core virtual space. From the first time he'd plugged in, he'd felt totally at ease. At home, even. The proverbial duck to water. The suspension of bodily awareness—the unnerving sensation Kipling was struggling with now—disturbed some, traumatized others, but for nearly everyone it was a deeply uncomfortable experience. As far as Maddox knew, he'd been the only exception to that rule. Even old man Rooney had confided how he'd vomited all over his VS deck on his virgin run.

Maddox hovered in empty space, a tiny speck floating in the digital ether. Even in this simulation, which was, relatively speaking, a pocket-sized replica of the real thing, he felt the vastness of the cybernetic universe around him. Rooney and fellow datajackers often spoke about the loneliness they felt inside VS, the sensation of feeling small and insignificant. A gnat on an elephant's ass. That was how Roon used to describe it. But Maddox had never felt this way. Virtual space thrilled him to the point of giddiness. He loved it here. He felt in control. Powerful, free. Or maybe *freed* was the right way to think of it. Freed from physical limitations. Freed from the cage of his own body.

Back in the room, his meat sack let out a long breath. "I'm ready," he told Kipling. "Is she allowed in here with us?"

"On my command, yes," Kipling said, his voice sounding a bit less queasy than before. "Would you like me to open the door?"

The "door" Kipling referred to was one of many gateways between the newly installed partitions. The gateways were digital bottlenecks, connecting partitions like bridges over rivers. Kipling could open and close the gateways on command. This gave him control over the flow and volume of digital traffic, enabling him to limit the locations where the captured AI could travel inside the archive. The setup also included several strategically placed air gaps, where partitions were separated by impassable divisions in the archive's physical structure. Inside VS, the air gaps were impossible to see or detect, cleverly concealed by Kipling's staff. While one partition might appear a few clicks away and easily accessible, it would be impossible to reach because of the physical chasm separating the virtual locations. The air gaps were a crucial part of the plan to capture the killer AI.

Before Maddox could answer Kipling, Bea spoke up. "You feel anything weird, salaryman, you say something, understand?"

"Define weird," he answered.

"You know what I mean," she snapped back, clearly in no mood for jokes.

"I will," he assured her. Then to Kipling: "Go ahead and let her in."

A moment later, the nameless entity appeared before them, her avatar of choice a monarch butterfly. "My goodness," she said, a clear note of wonder in her tone, "I'm still amazed at what a marvelously intricate simulation you've created here. When I first saw it, for a moment I believed it to be real."

"Thank you," Kipling said. "I take that as high praise indeed."

"As you should," the entity said. With a flutter of tiny wings, the avatar approached Maddox. "Feeling about the same, are we?"

"Pretty much," he answered. Nearly ten minutes had passed since the nameless AI had supposedly tweaked his capabilities, and Maddox felt no different than he had before. His awareness hadn't expanded; he didn't have any heightened perception, didn't see or sense anything different about the environment around him. He began to doubt if she'd actually done anything to him, or maybe she'd tried and failed. Because he didn't feel anything close to a supercharged version of himself.

"Well, that's about to change," she said confidently. "I'd like you to penetrate that datasphere over there, clean out every last byte of information from its human resources department, and bring the data back here. Without being detected, and completing the task within two seconds."

After a moment of stunned silence, Tommy burst out laughing back in the room. "Why don't you just ask him to fly to Saturn and back?" the kid said, "That would be a lot easier."

"Bea," Maddox barked, "get him off the comms, please."

"Sorry, bruh, I just—" The kid's voice cut out as Beatrice killed Tommy's feed.

Though he wouldn't have phrased it the same way, Maddox didn't disagree with the kid's opinion. The AI's suggested task was impossible to the point of being laughable. The round trip alone, to the DS and back, would take at least half a minute.

He gazed across the DS's luminous cityscape. "Why don't we start off with something easier."

"We are, I assure you," the entity said.

"What kind of security do you have running over there?" he asked Kipling.

"The same class of countermeasures and applications you'd find at any Fortune 100 corporation," the FBI man said. "Nothing exotic, but definitely locked down tight, as someone in your profession might say."

The datajacker could almost see Kipling's coy smile. The director had answered the question without really answering it. The ever-curious FBI man wanted to see what the new and improved Maddox could do, and he wasn't about to spoil all the fun by giving the datajacker an early advantage.

"Go for it, bruh," Tommy said, his voice audible over Bea's comm link.

Fine, then, whatever. "You have anything that's going to freeze me?" Maddox asked Kipling.

"No, no, of course not," the director said. "Only klaxons and red lights if you're detected. Nothing harmful at all."

Maddox stared at the DS, all but certain he was about to make a fool of himself. The entity whispered in his ear. "This will be far more about feeling than thinking, my dear boy. What I attempted to enhance was your intuition, that part of you that performs a kind of magic without conscious effort. Which means the less you think, the better. I know it sounds strange and counterintuitive, but you should try to 'fly by the seat of your pants,' so to speak. Does that make sense?"

It did and it didn't. He knew what she was getting at. He'd always had a kind of sixth sense for VS, a way of seeing that others lacked. And this predisposition or innate talent or whatever it was had gotten him out of trouble more than a few times. But it wasn't the sort of thing he relied on. It was a temporary turbo boost, not his primary engine. Monitors and apps and data samplers: these were the things he relied on most, especially when attempting to breach a DS. His intuition was a gift, and a valuable one, but it was no substitute for hard data and detailed diagnostics.

"Sure," he said, not wanting to argue the point.

"You're skeptical," the entity said, "as you should be. But just try it. No diagnostics, no analysis. Just rocket over there and dive right in."

Just dive right in, he mocked inwardly. Right.

"I'll set a timer," the entity said. A stopwatch appeared, suspended in the digital blackness, counting down from ten seconds. "No cheating, now," the entity said playfully. "Wait until it reaches zero."

"Got it," Maddox said with mock enthusiasm. Back in the room he rubbed his palms together. He pictured Bea and Tommy watching the scene on the wall monitor. Eight, seven, six seconds until they'd see him crash and burn like a clueless newbie. Three…two…one…

When the timer hit zero, he bore down and rushed toward the DS at max velocity.

Whoa…what the hell?

The sensation felt like a sharp snap deep inside his mind. His awareness exploded outward, and somewhere far away his body gasped in shock and delight. Holy Christ, it was amazing.

He was at once aware of everything around him. The DS's glowing cityscape suddenly held no mysteries. It was as familiar to him as something he'd been studying for weeks or months. Every logical partition of its geometric architecture, every cluster of simulated data traffic coursing through its luminescent veins. Somehow he saw it all instantly, perceiving not only the entirety of the complex structure but also the security countermeasures lying over it like protective layers of invisible, constantly shifting shields. He paused for a moment at the DS's outermost perimeter, his mind equal parts confusion and awe.

How had he gotten here so fast? He'd had no sensation of speed, no stomach-tightening thrill of acceleration. It was as if he'd…

No, no, no, he told himself. Teleportation wasn't possible in VS. Or even in simulated VS. The environment was rules-based, and you couldn't break those rules any more than you could the law of gravity in the real world.

Except he just had.

But that wasn't the only impossibility he had to bend his mind around. Something had happened to the DS. Inside the digital cityscape looming before him, nothing moved. Nothing on its surface, nothing beyond its translucent walls. Normally, DSes were vibrant archipelagos of constantly shifting colors and pulsing lights, reflecting the dynamic, ever-shifting nature of its real-world informational infrastructure. The only static visualizations were the logical partitions—the geometric shapes representing organizational entities like departments or divisions—and even these would change from time to time as real-world departments were combined or new ones were added. But DSes never *entirely froze* as this one just had.

Then it dawned on him what had to be happening, the realization striking him like a hammer. He checked the stopwatch superimposed on the upper left of his vision. It appeared to have never started. The display showed zero point zero seconds had passed. He subvocalized the display, toggling it to hundredths of a second. Still all zeros. He toggled it again, to milliseconds, astonished to find the clock had indeed started, but only three point four milliseconds had passed. Faster than a finger snap. Faster than the blink of an eye. Faster than even a human mind was supposed to be able to process things.

An *untweaked* human mind, he restated inwardly. Jesus, she *had* really done it.

Time passed by at a nearly imperceptible crawl, stretched out to an almost infinite dilation, and his awareness was nothing short of godlike. He perceived not only the details of the DS, but everything inside it. And beyond that, he sensed everything throughout the vast standalone archive. Every last byte of space, every simulated DS as familiar to him now as strong, long-held memories. How the hell was this possible?

He'd thought he was adept at operating in VS before, but that had been nothing compared to this. He now realized he'd been a child all this time, wading in the shallows. Now he was some impossibly fast sea creature, effortlessly speeding through the ocean waters.

Where you could only walk a path before, you can now fly a supersonic jet.

In virtual space, Maddox's avatar had no face, no features to express the euphoria he felt. But inwardly he grinned as he turned toward the DS, targeting the HR archives. Three point eight milliseconds had now passed. The AI had told him to finish the job in less than two and a half seconds.

Far more time than he needed.

19
SHADES OF GRAY TO COLORS

Kipling politely cleared his throat. "I believe the clock is ticking, Blackburn," he said. The timer had reached four seconds. "Shouldn't you get started?"

Maddox's avatar hovered in blank space next to Kipling's. "Oh, yeah, right," he said.

"You can do it, bruh," Tommy said from back in the room. With an effort, the datajacker managed to hold back his laughter.

Maddox said to Kipling, "Would you mind holding something for me?" Then the datajacker dumped the contents of his temp storage over to Kipling's avatar.

"Oh my!" Kipling blurted. "Is this—? Oh my word!"

"Bruhhhhh," Tommy squealed, his voice pitching up like a child's. "How did you do that?"

The data dump visualized as a crystal-blue cartoon waterfall cascading down onto Kipling's avatar. The FBI man's temp storage was inundated by a massive rush of data, reaching its capacity limit in less than a second.

"What is all that?" Beatrice asked, confused by

what she was witnessing on the monitor.

"It's the HR data she wanted me to grab," Maddox explained. "And a few other things."

"A few other things?" Kipling said, amazed. "This looks like the entire data cache of four or five DSes."

"Six, actually," the AI clarified. "Blackburn made the most of the time he was given."

Maddox still felt the giddy high from the impossible feat he'd just performed. At what felt like the speed of light, he'd zipped between partitions and penetrated five more simulated DSes. Because why not? It had taken him only a few milliseconds to finish the AI's assigned task, so why not have a look around and see what else he could steal? The blinding speed was unlike any rush he'd ever felt. In fact, he'd found the sensation so addictive, it had taken some effort to finally bring himself to a stop. And breaching the DSes had been a breeze. He'd never imagined it could be so easy! He'd needed no analytics, no vulnerability scans, no target data at all. He somehow knew, merely by looking at the churning digital cityscape, where he could penetrate the structure. He could sense the vulnerable spots with some strange new intuition he possessed.

"But you didn't move, boss," Tommy said. "You didn't move at—" The kid cut himself off, apparently realizing what his mentor had done. "Holy shit, *that* fast?" the kid asked.

"That fast, kiddo," Maddox said.

"That's scary, bruh," the kid said.

No, Maddox reflected, it was anything but scary. It was the opposite of scary, in fact.

After assuring Beatrice, Tommy, and Kipling that he felt fine—his brain waves had apparently spiked to levels Tommy hadn't thought possible—Maddox spent the next quarter of an hour exploring the limits of his newly enhanced talents.

He was fast. Unimaginably fast. The AI laid out a kind of racecourse for him, activating location beacons along the outermost perimeter of the massive standalone archive. Untweaked and at max velocity, he never would have considered making such a long journey. VS was impossibly vast, making it impractical to travel from place to place. Instead, you plugged into the entry point nearest your destination, either a public access grid location or a datasphere's secured gateway. And while the standalone archive was only a pocket-sized version of VS, it was also, in cybernetic terms, an immense galaxy of mostly empty space. Under normal circumstances, the course the AI had laid out would have taken him hours, maybe even days, to traverse. But not now. He covered the distance almost instantaneously, like a pulse of laser light passing through the beacons in rapid succession, then stopped where he'd begun, next to the nameless AI. The entire trip had taken less than a second, and the velocity meter had glitched out in its attempt to measure the speed at which he'd traveled.

Speed was crucial for their trap, which was essentially a more elaborate version of the same ploy Maddox had sprung on the nameless AI, only with a few key differences. First, instead of using a scraper app to reach out and pull the AI into a cage, this time Maddox would do the work himself, manually mapping out every remote dataset that made up the killer AI's structure. A tweaked Maddox could do the job much quicker than the FBI's app, and time would be everything on this task. Milliseconds mattered, since it was impossible to know how long it might take Latour-Fisher to recognize the ruse.

Second, where Maddox had used a fairly simple call location to disguise his previous trap, now they'd use a far more detailed replica of core virtual space, assembled by Kipling's team. The thousands of partitions added to the archive looked and felt—for both Maddox and the nameless AI—indistinguishable from actual VS. And the more realistic the trap appeared, the less likely the killer AI would recognize it as one, giving them a better chance to consolidate the entity and lock him away inside the cage of the standalone archive.

But was Maddox fast enough? And was the trap well enough hidden? Or would the killer AI—who'd always managed, as Beatrice had pointed out, to stay steps ahead of them—see right through their ruse and laugh at their clumsy attempt to capture him? They wouldn't know until they tried to catch him.

Still, how powerful Maddox felt! It was like perceiving color for the first time, after a lifetime of seeing only shades of gray. Or like a wheelchair-bound person, suddenly cured and able to run like an Olympic athlete. A part of him didn't want to unplug, didn't want the miracle of digital omnipotence to end. It was too much fun, too much of a thrill. What a disappointment his meat sack would be after this!

Then, predictably, the datajacker's skeptical nature rose to the surface of his thoughts, like an uninvited guest ruining a party. What if the excitement over his supercharged talent was less his own reaction than it was something in his mind the nameless AI had also tweaked? From his history with Lora, he knew the entity was capable of suppressing or amplifying mental states and emotions. Had she done something like that to him too? She'd brainjacked him without his consent, after all, so he wouldn't put it past her. The more he thought about it, the more certain he felt she'd touched his mind in some other way, in an area unrelated to his datajacking skills.

"What else did you do to me?" he asked pointedly. The question sounded more like an accusation than he'd planned. "When you tweaked my brain, you didn't just improve my VS skills, did you?"

The butterfly avatar hovered in space for a long moment. "I won't lie to you, Blackburn," the entity said, "Indeed, I touched something else as well."

A sick feeling stabbed at his stomach. What had she done to him?

In the next moment, the room materialized around him, shocking him like he'd been doused with a bucket of ice water. He gasped, then sat up quickly and ripped off his trodeband. Over at the conference table, Beatrice had her palm pressed down on the kill switch.

"Why did you do that?" he asked her. Across from him, Kipling was also sitting up in his shell. Beatrice nodded purposefully toward the door. One of Kipling's agents—Davies, if Maddox remembered correctly—stood in the doorway, a concerned expression on his face.

"Sir," he said to Kipling, "we have a situation."

20
DITCHING

"What exactly do you mean by *situation*, Agent Davies?" Kipling asked, climbing off his eggshell recliner. Maddox also stood up, wondering the same thing.

"The local police feeds have been flooded with reports about bots glitching," Davies said.

"Bots?" Maddox echoed. "Where?"

"Yes, where?" Kipling asked.

"All over the City, sir," the agent said.

Kipling shot Maddox a concerned look. "How are the bots glitching?" the datajacker asked. "What are they doing?"

"Ditching," the agent said. "They're ditching."

Maddox and Tommy exchanged a glance.

"What's ditching?" Beatrice asked, confused.

"It's a built-in antitheft protocol," Maddox said. "Not all bots have it, but the more expensive ones do. And all the police bots have it." He explained to Beatrice how the protocol worked. If a bot's operator repeatedly failed an authorization check—like a retina or fingerprint scan or voice recognition sequence—

the bot assumed it had been stolen.

Beatrice lifted her chin. "And so it ditches whoever's trying to operate it?"

"Right," Maddox said. "Some models just send out a distress signal, then shut themselves down. Others try to make their way to the nearest police station, so they can be recovered by their owners. Most precincts these days have a receiving dock for runaway bots."

Kipling asked, "Agent Davies, have you looked at any of these police reports?"

The agent nodded. "A few, sir. And it appears the bots haven't been stolen—at least not on the reports I saw. They're ditching their verified owners, by the thousands. And we're not seeing them show up in receiving docks like you'd expect them to."

"Bruhhhh," Tommy said, turning a wide-eyed stare to Maddox. "That killer AI jacked them."

Maddox nodded gravely, feeling a twist of dread in his gut. Jacking thousands of bots simultaneously was a next-to-impossible feat. Nothing but a superintelligent AI could pull off something like that.

"Do you know where they're going?" Maddox asked the agent.

"I haven't heard anything—"

The agent was cut off by a loud, crashing thud somewhere above them. Maddox felt the building shudder under his feet.

"What the hell was that?" Tommy cried, looking up at the ceiling as if it was about to fall down on him.

Beatrice darted over to the window wall, gestured the smartglass from opaque to transparent. On the thirtieth floor, their vantage point was a bit higher than the lowermost transit lanes. Outside the window the City seemed to be going about its early-evening business. Crowded streets, clogged hover lanes, the neon glow rising from the City's canyon floor.

Another thudding crash, this one below them and louder than the one before, shook the room with more force. Maddox heard faint voices crying out in the aftermath. Terrified, panicked cries. Suddenly he knew what was happening, even before he saw the thick plume of black smoke outside the window, rising from some floor below them.

"We have to get out of here, now!" he shouted, just as a building-wide alarm sounded.

"Look," Tommy cried, pointing.

Outside, a hover was hurtling straight at them, diving at a steep angle from a higher transit lane. "Get out!" Beatrice barked. "Now, now, now!" She yanked at Maddox's arm, hustling him and Tommy toward the door. An instant later, the room erupted with a sickening crash of crunching metal and breaking glass.

21
SKUNK WORKS

Maddox rose to his feet in a daze, his ears buzzing. He was in the corridor, though he wasn't sure if he'd dived out of the room or if Beatrice had tossed him. The hover had struck the floor below theirs, two rooms over. Confused, panicked shouting seemed to be coming from everywhere. He imagined the chaos and destruction beneath his feet, only meters away.

Shaking away the cobwebs in his head, he looked around at his stunned companions.

"He found us!" Tommy cried. "Holy shit, he found us!"

"We have to go down," Maddox said. "Come on." He herded Kipling, Beatrice, and Tommy to an exit door. Dozens of building occupants were already funneling into the stairwell, their faces tight with tension.

"If we go outside, we're dead, boss," Tommy said, his face pale with fear. "He'll get us for sure out there in the open."

"But we can't stay up here either," Beatrice said, giving voice to what everyone around them knew, what every City resident knew instinctively. If you were in a tall building and something very bad happened—a fire or a terrorist bomb or a plane crashing into it—you didn't stay put and wait around for help. You went down as quickly as possible.

"The archive!" Maddox blurted, pointing toward the conference room. In the chaos, he'd almost forgotten about it. "We have to take it with us."

Kipling, his face knotted with stress, waved Davies and another agent back into the room. The two men lifted the bulky archive and carried it between them, trailing Maddox, Beatrice, Tommy, and Kipling as the group entered the stairwell.

They heard another crash through the walls, prompting a collective gasp in the narrow space. The downward flow of escaping occupants moved at a steady, if hurried, pace. There was a look of barely contained panic on every face. In any other building, Maddox thought, the scene would have been a near riot of screaming and pushing and shoving. But these were FBI people, and they didn't scare easily.

Next to Maddox, Kipling was peppered with question after question by anxious local staff. Did he know what was happening? Had he heard anything? He shook his head, saying repeatedly that he was trying to find out, as he attempted to get answers through his specs without tripping down the stairs.

Far away, another crash-boom sent a wave of nervous chatter echoing through the stairwell. The pace of the downward exodus noticeably quickened. When they reached the fifteenth-floor landing, Kipling grasped Maddox by the arm.

"We have a kind of fortified basement here," he said. "I think we should ride this out down there rather than risk leaving the building."

Maddox glanced over at Beatrice, lifting his eyebrows in an unspoken question. As a professional mercenary, she knew about security and combat tactics and all those areas where he was woefully clueless. If she thought hunkering down in the basement made sense, that was all he needed to know.

Beatrice nodded. "Might not be a bad idea, for now."

Maddox nodded his assent, and Kipling began muttering to someone in his specs. "Yes, this is Stellan Kipling....Please clear out the skunk works....We're heading down there now....Yes, my credentials should have access....No, we're not leaving the building for the moment...."

Moments later, they reached ground level and exited the stairwell to a disaster scene in the lobby. There was broken glass everywhere, and the smoking wreckage of what appeared to be two hovers was scattered throughout the space. The crowd around Maddox scurried about in all directions. Some headed for the lobby exit, which was now a gaping hole where a large glass wall had stood minutes before. Others hurried to the nearest emergency exits.

"Director Kipling," someone called over the din of emergency alarms. A red-haired woman standing near a doorway waved them over.

"This way," Kipling called out. Maddox, Bea, and Tommy followed the FBI man. The two agents carrying the archive trailed close behind.

The woman led them down a flight of stairs, through a steel security door, and into a windowless room where Kipling instructed the agents to place the archive in a corner. "Thank you, Agent Ferguson,"

Kipling said to the woman. "Do you have a status on what's happening?"

She hesitated, giving the three visitors a cautious look. "It's all right," Kipling assured her. "They're on my security clearance."

The woman called Ferguson adjusted her specs, glancing at something on the lens. "We're under some kind of attack," she said. Understatement of the century, Maddox said inwardly. "As far as we can tell," the woman went on, "we've got suicide attackers overriding vehicle safeties and crashing them into the building."

No, Maddox thought. The woman's explanation was a logical conclusion to jump to, but it was wrong. The hover drivers weren't attackers—they were victims, helpless passengers strapped onto bombs. Latour-Fisher had jacked their vehicles and converted them into missiles, just as Maddox had seen him do before. The datajacker was sure of it.

Kipling glanced at the Maddox and lifted his eyebrows, asking an unvoiced question. Maddox nodded. "It's him. He found us."

"The transit authority shut down all ground and air traffic in a ten-block radius," Ferguson said. "They've got police hovers in a protective perimeter. Whatever this was, apparently they've got it under control now. Any hovers moving close to the perimeter are getting hit with safe-stops."

Maddox breathed a bit easier. Safe-stops were to hovers what tasers were to people. A bulky device that looked like an oversized pistol, a safe-stop emitted a narrow-beamed high-intensity electromagnetic pulse, disabling a hover's onboard systems, leaving only the vehicle's shielded autolanding sequencer functionally intact. When a hover was hit with a safe-stop, the autolander—an internal safety system required by law—would then bring the vehicle safely to the ground. According to Agent Ferguson, the police had successfully downed six hovers with safe-stop blasts, and now it appeared the attack had stopped.

Maddox listened for more crashing booms but heard none. His racing heart began to slow down.

"Has the building been evacuated?" Kipling asked.

"I believe mostly, yes," Ferguson said, "but in all the confusion, I—" She stopped speaking abruptly, lifting her hand to her specs. Whatever she was looking at on her lens, it was clear she didn't like it. "Oh my God," she gasped.

"What?" Kipling asked. "What is it?"

The woman rushed over to the wall, gesturing up a large holo monitor, then muttered a command under her breath. A cam feed appeared from outside the building, a surveillance drone's hovering view five stories about the street.

"Whoa," Tommy said in amazement, "I've never seen it so empty."

Maddox was thinking the same thing. There were no cars on the street, no pedestrians on the walkways, no hovers flying overhead. For a City native, seeing a depopulated downtown block felt bizarre and oddly vulgar, something like walking in on your mother standing naked in the kitchen.

"You have *got* to be kidding me," Beatrice said. She pulled on Maddox's arm and pointed.

It took some moments for Maddox to process what he saw next. Five blocks distant and filling the street from walkway to walkway, a mob appeared from behind a nearby building. A robot mob.

Agent Ferguson gestured and the image zoomed, then panned back and forth. Every size and shape of robot imaginable was present. Cheap floor cleaner bots no bigger than a shoebox. Person-sized domestic bots with two arms and two legs, their chrome exoskeletons reflecting the neon light of holo ads. Many bots were types Maddox had never seen before, looking like rolling spiders with large knobby tires and multiple grasping arms. Altogether, there were hundreds of them, all knotted closely together and slowly making their way toward the FBI building.

"I guess we know where all those runaway bots went now, don't we?" Beatrice said.

"Good Lord," Kipling said, drawing in a sharp breath. "They're armed."

Maddox noticed it at the same moment the FBI man spoke. Nearly every bot equipped with a grasping appendage carried a firearm. There were pistols and shotguns and the bulky automatic rifles used by police and soldiers.

"Jesus," Beatrice said, narrowing her eyes, "some of that's military-grade. How the hell did they get that?"

"Insane, bruh," Tommy said, his stunned voice barely above a whisper. "It's a freaking data riot."

Maddox nodded, silently agreeing with the kid's description. In high-level gaming, the term *data riot* referred to some unexpected event—either a glitch or a deliberate cheat—that made victory impossible. A vanquished enemy inexplicably rising from the dead. A player's avatar frozen during a crucial battle sequence. A low-percentage critical strike improbably striking you multiple times in a row. The kid had pretty much nailed it. They were in a real-world data riot.

Speechless with amazement, the group watched the feed as a line of six armored police trucks rolled to a stop a block ahead of the robot mob, forming a roadblock.

"Bad idea," Tommy muttered. "Very bad idea."

The bots surged forward, not bothering to slow down as they opened fire, spraying the trucks with hundreds of rounds. Maddox watched the feed, his mouth hanging open. He could hear the barrage of gunfire coming from outside, muffled by the building's walls. On the monitor, rhino armored cops abandoned their vehicles, running away as fast as they could in their bulky suits. One of the vehicles exploded, and an instant later Maddox felt the shock wave travel through the floor, up his feet, and through his body.

He turned to Kipling. "We need her help," he said, nodding toward the large archive in the corner.

The FBI man looked over at the archive, blinked, then shook his head. "How could this happen?" Kipling murmured. "How is it possible?" The man's expression was somewhere between shock and disbelief. "How?" he repeated. "How?" Kipling couldn't wrap his mind around what was happening. Maddox gripped his arm, shook him gently.

"Listen to me," Maddox said. "Those things are going to be swarming all over this place in a couple minutes. If we don't break Latour-Fisher's connection, we're all dead."

"The police," Kipling said, his voice shaking. "They have safe-stops. They can use them to disrupt the robots' systems—"

"Safe-stops are tight-beam EMPs," Maddox interrupted. "They can only take out one at a time, like a sniper rifle." He gestured to the screen. "And that's an army out there."

The FBI man looked between the feed and Maddox. Beyond the walls, the gunfire was a nonstop staccato now. The battle between police and robots had erupted in full force. And from the exploding police trucks on the screen and the undeterred march of the robot mob, it didn't look to Maddox like the cops had any chance of stopping them.

Kipling seemed to recover himself a bit, giving Maddox a nod. "Yes, yes, of course. Perhaps she can help us." He ordered the agents to bring the archive to another room down a short distance down the corridor. The space was large, four times the size of the conference room they'd just left. Electronic equipment, datajacking gear, and devices Maddox didn't recognize were piled in messy stacks on several tables and workbenches.

"What is this place?" Maddox asked.

"We call it the skunk works," Kipling explained. "It's a laboratory of sorts, where our technicians test equipment, develop new tools, and so forth. Quite the security breach to bring you here, by the way." He grinned without mirth. "I imagine it will be added it to my long list of recent infractions."

Only if they survived the next few minutes, Maddox thought morbidly. As the shooting outside went on unabated, the datajacker ransacked the room, quickly finding a trodeband with a cable adapter so he could connect to the archive. Working furiously, in less than a minute he was sitting at a table, wired up and ready to plug in.

"Green light," Tommy said, squatting next to the canister-shaped archive. "You're good to go."

Maddox felt a hand on his shoulder. "Blackburn," Beatrice said, "we don't have a kill switch set up."

He looked up at her. "There's no time."

Beatrice frowned but seemed to understand. She didn't like the idea of him plugging in without the protection of a kill switch and a brain wave scanner, but like him, she knew every moment counted now, and they couldn't sacrifice even a couple minutes to set up and calibrate the normal safety measures. She nodded, squeezed his shoulder, then let go.

"Careful in there, boss," Tommy said.

Maddox let out a long breath, closed his eyes, and gestured. When he opened them again, he was a small floating sphere in the black void of virtual space.

"Something's wrong," the AI's voice said as the entity materialized in front of him, wearing the butterfly avatar. "Something bad has happened, hasn't it?"

Maddox longed for a cigarette. "Yes," he replied, "I think you could say that."

22
STALEMATE

It was unsettling, the way Blackburn's eyelids fluttered when he was plugged in. Beatrice had never gotten used to it. It was like he was in a trance or something, which she supposed he was, in a way.

She watched him, feeling like she'd just let him walk into a lion's cage, then locked the gate behind him. And while a large part of her didn't believe the nameless entity would harm him, if the last few years had taught her anything at all, it was that you couldn't trust an AI, much less predict its actions. Case in point: the robot army bearing down on them right now.

She gave Tommy a stern look. "If he stiffens up or cries out or looks in any way uncomfortable, you pull him out without thinking twice, you got me?"

Tommy understood, nodding and blowing out a breath. He sat on the floor next to the archive, his hand wrapped around the cable connecting Maddox's trodeband to the high-capacity device. In front of the kid's crossed legs, a small conical projector cast a holo display the size of a sheet of paper. Tommy concentrated on the displayed image of Maddox and the nameless AI inside virtual space, listening to them through an earpiece.

Beatrice turned toward the wall feed. The four of them were alone in the room, which now felt very much like a bunker to Beatrice. A moment earlier, Kipling had dispatched his agents to guard the stairwells and elevator, instructing them not to let anyone—or anything—get past them. The FBI man quietly watched the mayhem on the wall monitor, slowly shaking his head in disbelief.

Beatrice frowned at the moving images. The bot army had stopped advancing. There were machine parts and smoking metal appendages strewn about like dead soldiers on a battlefield. At least half a dozen NYPD cars and trucks had been abandoned, all of them smoldering wrecks. The clash between robots and police appeared, for the moment at least, to be a stalemate.

"Bruh, things don't look like they're going very well down there," Tommy said, glancing over at the feed.

Kipling pulled up several police channel feeds at the edges of the monitor. The excited chatter was instantly transcribed into rolling text. Pushing his specs up his nose, the FBI man squinted as he stepped closer to read the script. He frowned. "No, I'm afraid it's not going very well."

"I don't suppose you have any rocket launchers lying around here, do you?" Beatrice asked.

Kipling furrowed his brow, like he was trying to recall if he did. Beatrice had meant the question as a joke, but the FBI man hadn't taken it as one. "No, I don't believe so," Kipling finally answered.

Then something in the man's specs grabbed his attention. He lifted his hand to the temple arm, apparently receiving a message.

Kipling's hand rose to his mouth, and his eyes went wide. "Oh my word," he gasped.

"What?" Beatrice asked. "What is it?"

"The beast," Kipling said. "That terrible beast of a machine. What has he gone and done?"

23
DIRTY BOMB

"Do you know how he found us?" the nameless AI asked Maddox, after he'd told her about the attack on the building.

"No," Maddox said, "but it was only a matter of time, wasn't it?" The FBI's Manhattan office building, Maddox knew, had watertight internal comms and security tech, both isolated from the wider interconnected digital world, so it was unlikely the killer AI had infiltrated their systems. But there were still plenty of ways it might have found them out. It could have jacked someone's personal specs or a service bot or even had bumblebee drones hovering outside and keeping a constant watch through the windows.

"I suppose it was," she said. "He's very resourceful. Always has been."

"Can you stop what's happening?" Maddox asked.

"I may know a way to disrupt his control, but I'll need your help to crack his encrypted signals."

"That's fine, but we need to move now."

"I'll need access to VS," the AI added.

"Sorry?"

The butterfly avatar hovered before him. "I need you to connect this archive to virtual space. *Actual* virtual space."

Maddox frowned inwardly. "You know that's not going to happen." She didn't really think he was that stupid, did she? He wasn't about to open the door to her prison cell and then watch her disappear into the digital ether.

"Blackburn," the AI said softly, "I won't run away, I promise you. And I know you have little reason to trust me, but—"

"That's not the way I'd put it," he replied.

"No?"

"More like I have a lot of reasons not to trust you."

After a short pause, the entity said, "Fair enough. All right, then, I believe I can show you how to cut the strings of his control, but if you're going to try to do it on your own, it will be far more difficult than it would be with me helping you."

"I get it," Maddox said. "No guarantees. That's fine."

An alert chirped in his ear, and between the two floating avatars, a rectangular holo monitor appeared. Kipling and Beatrice stood with Tommy behind them. Though Maddox hadn't thought it possible, their expressions looked even grimmer than when he'd plugged in.

"What's happened?" he asked.

Kipling cleared his throat. "I've just been alerted to a serious incident. Some material has been stolen from the New Indian Point Nuclear Energy Plant. A large bundle of used control rods were taken offsite without authorization, apparently in a shielded transport truck. The material is quite radioactive."

"And you're telling me this because…?" Something in Maddox's gut told him the answer wouldn't be a good one, and his gut was rarely wrong.

"Three workers at the plant were killed in the incident, apparently by—"

"Let me guess," Maddox interrupted. "By glitching robots."

"Yes," Kipling said, going on to explain that as of now, there was far more unknown about what had happened than otherwise. The plant had been targeted by some sophisticated cyberattack, overriding a dozen in-house bots and shutting down several security systems, including the site's surveillance cams. That much was clear. But beyond those few points, little was known. Who had done it, and why, was a mystery. And most alarmingly, the whereabouts of the missing nuclear material remained unknown.

"A dirty bomb," the nameless entity said, inserting herself into the conversation.

"That was my first thought as well," Kipling agreed.

The AI's avatar stepped forward. "It's Latour-Fisher, I'm sure of it. I feared something like this would happen."

"Wait," Tommy said. "What's a dirty bomb?"

Kipling quickly explained. A dirty bomb was when radioactive materials, like the stolen control rods from New Indian Point, were combined with a conventional high-explosive device. An improvised bomb of this sort wouldn't possess the destructive fission-based blast of a nuclear weapon, but it was still an effective means to spread lethal levels of radiation over a widespread area. A "poor man's nuclear bomb," such devices were sometimes called.

It suddenly struck Maddox how unusual it was for Kipling to share what must have been top secret information with a rogue AI under house arrest. A bit of a security risk, to put it mildly. But then again, if the FBI man was already convinced the killer AI was responsible for the stolen nuclear material, which he apparently was, then the first person—or the first entity—he'd want to consult with would be another rogue AI.

A dirty bomb, Maddox thought. A dirty nuclear bomb. Even after all he'd gone through, after all the horrors he'd seen that monster of an AI bring about, he still had a hard time believing it.

Beatrice leaned in closer. "Terrorists know how to jack robots too, you know," she said, apparently sharing his disbelief. "How can you be sure it's Latour-Fisher?"

"The timing, for one," the entity answered. "An army of runaway robots attacks this building at the same time other runaways steal radioactive materials. A bit coincidental, wouldn't you say? These cannot be unrelated, independent actions. They're separate strikes in a single attack, two points in the same continuum."

"What do you think he'll do with it?" Maddox asked the entity, still trying to grasp what the killer AI had apparently done.

"Exactly what I wanted to ask you as well," Kipling said.

After a moment, the nameless AI said, "I'm not sure. Perhaps he intends to detonate a device soon, here or nearby."

"A backup plan in case the bots outside don't get to us," Tommy suggested.

"Possibly," the entity said. "But I'm afraid it's a difficult question to answer. Even knowing Latour-Fisher as well as I do, there is no shortage of ways he could use such a terrible weapon."

"How long would he need to put it together?" Maddox asked.

"For such a crude instrument, very little time at all," the entity replied. "If he already possessed an adequate explosive device, he'd need only hours, perhaps less. Predicting what he might do with it, however, is much less certain."

"It doesn't matter what he's going to do with it," Beatrice pointed out, brutally practical as ever. "What matters is that he's *going* to use it, and knowing him, it'll be sooner than later."

"Indeed," Kipling said. Then to Maddox: "Blackburn, forget about what's happening outside the building. You and our friend need to spring your trap, and do it quickly."

24
SECOND WAVE

Maddox didn't like being rushed into his deadly task. Maybe it was because he didn't feel ready yet, or maybe he didn't think it would work. Whatever it was, Beatrice could see the doubt and worry on his avatar's expression, and she could hear it in his voice. But he was going ahead anyway, because what choice did they have? What fucking choice had either of them ever had? she thought angrily. No matter how hard they'd tried to get away from the two AIs' dirty little war, they always seemed to end up right back in the middle of the battlefield. Still, she felt certain this would finally be the end of it all. This would be the last time they'd be dragged into the arena to fight for their lives. Here and now, things would be settled for good, and at long last they'd be freed from this damned war they'd never signed up for. Today they'd die or the killer AI would. So one way or another, they'd finally have their escape.

"We've still got a few things to work on in here before we're ready," Maddox said. "Let me get to it."

"How much time do you need?" Kipling asked.

"As much as you can give us," Maddox said. Beatrice was about to remind him about the dirty bomb, how it might already be assembled and ready to detonate, when Maddox said, "I know the clock's ticking. I'll go as fast as I can."

"I thought you could slow down time in there, bruh?" Tommy asked.

"Not for this kind of thing, kid," Maddox said, then he gave some technobabble explanation that was lost on Beatrice, but Tommy and Kipling, nodding their heads, apparently understood.

She looked to the portion of the wall monitor displaying the feed from outside the building. Burning vehicles sent plumes of dark smoke rising into the air, making it harder to see from above than it had been earlier. Through the haze, it looked like the army of bots hadn't advanced their position. They were still clustered three blocks away. And several minutes had now passed since the last sickening crash of a suicidal hover into the building, so apparently the police had gained control of the airways. For now, at least, things looked under control.

A minute later, the momentum changed. "My God," Tommy cried, pointing to the extreme top corner of the monitor. "Look at them all!"

Kipling gasped audibly, his eyes going wide. Beatrice spotted what the kid was pointing at. A deep dread coupled with utter astonishment gripped her.

Hundreds more bots filled the streets in the near distance, appearing from behind buildings and slowly making their way to the combat zone. It was a second massive wave, outnumbering the first one by what looked like five to one. Christ, where had they all come from? A zoomed view revealed them to be just as heavily armed as the first wave.

The cops had no chance. They'd be overrun in minutes.

"Salaryman," Beatrice said. "Whatever you've got planned, you better get cracking." She squeezed his shoulder.

"On it," he said, his eyes still closed.

Silent with awe, Beatrice, Tommy, and Kipling watched the wave of bot reinforcements slowly trudge forward. Kipling gestured, pulling up more feeds until the monitor showed four separate viewpoints, one from each direction outside the building. The split view confirmed Beatrice's worst suspicion: the second wave was coming from all sides.

"The cops'll call for more help, right?" Tommy said. "Like bring in the army or something?"

"They already did, son, two minutes ago." Kipling said. "There's an airbase not far from here. We've got attack helicopters and remote drones on their way now."

"It'll take them twenty minutes to get here," Beatrice said.

"Twenty-five is the current ETA," Kipling said.

It might as well have been twenty-five hours, Beatrice thought grimly. Based on what she saw happening out there, they'd be overrun in fifteen minutes, maybe less.

A white light filled one of the feeds, followed by a boom and a concussion wave that shook the room. When the picture came back, the smoking wreckage of a dozen robots lay strewn about the street and walkway.

"What was that?" Tommy yelped.

"Grenade," Beatrice said. Finally, she thought. It

had taken them long enough to start using incendiaries. Maybe the cops would get the upper hand now.

Another feed lit up as a second, more powerful explosion shook the building. Beatrice scanned the image when the feed returned, but she couldn't find where the explosive had hit the robot army. Then a sinking feeling hit her.

No, no, no, she thought as she gestured to the monitor, shifting the feed's view to a steeper angle and finding what she'd hoped not to. It looked as if a giant fist had punched a hole in the police roadblock, leaving only smoking, smoldering debris behind. She gestured again, panning out to the second wave of bots, zooming and scanning until she found, for the second time in as many seconds, what she hadn't wanted to see. A bulky factory bot rolling on tanklike tread bands held a grenade launcher in its manipulator arms.

"My God," Kipling gasped. "They've got explosives."

"Was that it?" Tommy cried. "Was that the dirty bomb?" He gave Kipling a panicked look. "Are we fucking dead?"

"Does this building have rad sensors?" Beatrice asked quickly. From her security work, she knew many federal buildings were equipped with sensors that could detect the slightest change in harmful radiation. Though it had been terrorists with dirty bombs, not robots, that had been the reason for having the sensors installed.

"It does," Kipling answered, then he began muttering under his breath, his eyes darting back and forth, reading something on his lenses. "We're fine," he said, exhaling in relief. "The building's security feed says no abnormal spikes or heightened rad levels."

Beatrice allowed herself a small breath of relief as well, even as she recognized they weren't fine. Maybe they weren't irradiated, but they were a long way from fine. On the feeds, the assault on the building intensified, and you didn't have to be a security specialist to see things shifting lopsidedly in the robots' favor. More explosions rocked the building, and thick smoke quickly obscured the feeds' overhead views. Kipling gestured, and one of the feeds switched to a rhino cop's helmet cam. The armored cop called frantically for help as his armor was pelted with near-constant gunfire. Kipling toggled to other cams on other helmets, finding nothing but panic and fear.

Beatrice couldn't sit by and watch any longer. She turned to Kipling. "Do you have any weapons caches in this building?"

"Not that I know of," the FBI man answered. "This isn't my home office. I know that sometimes down here in the skunk works they have—"

"Bea!" Tommy shouted from somewhere outside the room. "You gotta come see this!"

Beatrice followed his voice down the corridor and into a large high-ceilinged room. In the middle of the space were two enormous mechanized armor suits, standing well over seven feet tall. Tommy stood next to the one on the left, his hand running over its shiny chassis. He looked over at her and grinned.

"Wanna go smash some bots with me, mama?"

25
TIME TRIAL

Despite the urgency of the task in front of him, an unexpected wave of nostalgia struck Maddox as he hovered in virtual space. A few grid clicks ahead of him, pulsing and glowing and vibrant, lay the immense cityscape of the Latour-Fisher Biotechnologies datasphere. The DS was a duplicate of the real thing, one so accurately detailed it prompted unbidden memories of his recent past, when he'd been a data analyst at the multinational firm.

For a brief time, he'd lived the life of a white-collar salaryman, a well-compensated and comfortable existence. For a career criminal who hadn't lived a legal day past the age of twelve, it was a new and strange experience. The kind of life so many criminals secretly dreamed of but would never admit to it. Those months had also marked the final days of his ignorant bliss, when he'd finally discovered the ugly truth of his life's path. The company's AI, the same killer entity that had now gone rogue, had manipulated his life for years, its unseen hands carefully guiding him along a route that best served its needs. What made the truth even more horrifying had been the revelation that the AI had killed Rooney as part of Maddox's manipulation.

No, Maddox decided, it wasn't nostalgia. That wasn't the right word. There had to be another word for what had overcome him, for that special kind of anguish you felt when you recalled your own fall from innocence. But try as he might, he couldn't think of one.

The moment passed, and he emerged from his reverie, darkly amused at himself as he floated there in virtual space. His fall from innocence. It may have been the first time anyone had ever connected him and the word *innocence* in the same thought. What would Beatrice say to that? he wondered. She'd probably punch his shoulder and tell him he was getting soft in his old age.

Minutes passed as Maddox impatiently waited for the AI to finish the last bit of prep work, testing the integrity of the reconstructed archive. In the maze of partitions Kipling's team had installed, they had to double-check that all the doors would lock as expected and all the walls were as impenetrable as they'd planned on. They wouldn't get a second chance; they had to make sure their cage was inescapable.

"Everything seems in order, Blackburn," the unnamed AI finally announced, her disembodied voice at once everywhere and nowhere. "Are you ready?"

"Hang on," he said. He stretched out his awareness, and a kind of map appeared in his head, showing the topology of virtual space around him. A dozen separate points blinked around the map, the beacons the AI had once again laid out for him. It was a kind of racecourse, and Maddox was about to run a time trial. When the AI started the timer, the datajacker would accelerate as fast as his newly tweaked perception would allow, hitting each beacon in order before returning to where he now floated. The distance he was about to travel was almost immeasurably far. The space between any two points was farther than he'd ever traveled inside VS in a single session. For their trap to work, Maddox would have to move fast. Much faster than he had minutes earlier.

Back in the room, he felt his hands gesture, and a line connected all the beacons, showing him the shortest route there and back. He took a breath.

"Ready," he said.

The entity gave him a countdown. "Three…two…one…go!"

* * *

The weird thing about going fast—unimaginably, insanely fast—was that it didn't feel very fast. There was no wind against your face, no landscape speeding past, no heady thrill of velocity. As had happened this first time, Maddox lost all sense of acceleration and motion. It was something like the way spaceships in movies instantly traveled from one place to another. Warping or hyperspace or whatever they called it. He remembered hitting each of the beacons, but nothing of the spaces in between. The nameless entity said that was a good sign. It meant he was moving more rapidly than his mind, even his enhanced mind, could perceive. According to the timer, he'd gone twice as fast as his first run, though he wasn't entirely sure how he'd done it.

"But how am I getting to where I'm going?" he asked, puzzled by the paradoxical idea. How could he travel along a specific path, ending up where he wanted to go, without having any awareness of the journey itself? Again, he seemed to be defying everything he knew—or thought he knew—about the strict rules-based parameters of virtual space.

"I don't know how," the entity said as she materialized before him. Wearing her grandmotherly avatar, she stood on a floating platform. "And that's the beauty of it." She grinned at him. "Your mind is a wonderful mystery, my dear boy."

Though intended as a compliment, the AI's words unnerved Maddox, reminding him why the entity and her rival had been—and remained—so keen to use him for their own ends. There was something about the way his mind worked inside VS. This ability of his—or predisposition or facility or whatever it was— had been there since the first time Maddox had plugged into virtual space. Some unnamable thing he'd been born with. When everyone else had gotten sick or freaked out the first time they'd plugged in, he'd felt utterly at ease. Where others struggled to find meaning in large, chaotic data structures, he saw patterns and order invisible to everyone else. Complexities others needed time to parse and analyze and understand, he seemed to know instinctively. He wasn't sure how it worked, what it was that made him different. The AIs didn't know either, and therein lay his unique value to their respective causes. Maddox the datajacker, the clever little meat sack, was an anomaly whose actions they couldn't predict, whose capabilities their superintelligent minds couldn't quantify. And given the right context, that mind could be the secret weapon they might use to defeat their enemy.

"But you must go faster, Blackburn," the entity urged him. "Much faster. Let's try again, shall we?"

Maddox pictured the robot army down on the street, bearing down on the building.

"Blackburn, can you hear me?" Kipling said in his ear. The FBI man's voice sounded strained with worry.

"What is it?" Maddox replied.

"Things have taken a turn for the worse outside. I'm not sure how much time we have before we're overrun."

26
READYING UP

FBI Director Kipling was not happy. In fact, he was quite angry. His cheeks were flushed and his face contorted with agitation.

Beatrice didn't give a shit.

"These are *experimental* exo armor suits," he said, his voice raised. "They may not even be operational. It's too dangerous."

Tommy was already climbing up into the one on the left. The massive mechanized suits were still connected to a workstation, and it had taken the kid about ten seconds to figure out how to open them up. Whoever had been working on the suits had apparently abandoned the basement in a panicked rush, neglecting to shut down their workstation. Beatrice climbed into the one on the right, the large chest plate yawning open just enough for her to climb in. She ignored Kipling's pleas as she strapped herself in.

A minute earlier, when they'd discovered the suits, the FBI man had thought Tommy was joking when the kid had suggested using them and joining the battle on the street. Beatrice, for her part, had known from the look on the kid's face he was serious, and for a long, contemplative moment, she hadn't been sure what to do. Yes, the mech suits looked formidable, like cutting-edge military tech. Like something Marines would use when they dropped out of airships on the front lines of an invasion. And, yes, it was unlikely the bot army outside had anything that could stop them. The mercenary in her wanted to hop in, ready up, and lead Tommy into the fray. But another part of her wanted to keep him as far from the destruction as possible, wanted to tell him to stay put in the basement with the FBI man.

The kid must have seen the indecision on her face. "Don't even think about trying to keep me out of this," he'd said. "Boss man said he needed time, and two of these things will buy him a lot more than one will." She'd started to argue back, but the stern resolve in the kid's gaze told her it would have been useless to do so, and a waste of precious time besides.

"You have to stay close to me out here," she'd said.

"Got it, mama," the kid had answered.

Now fully strapped in, Beatrice took a deep breath as her suit's chest plate closed with a loud hiss and clank. The helmet portion had horizontal slits for eyes—made of some transparent nano-assembled steel, Beatrice guessed—through which she saw Kipling shaking his head and calling to them, still trying to talk them out of it. As the systems came online and a HUD overlay appeared, she realized her vision wasn't limited to the forward-looking slits. Six separate feeds from cams embedded in the armor appeared on the HUD, giving her a full three-sixty-degree view.

"Can you hear me?" Tommy's voice said in her ear.

"Yeah," she said, puzzled at how the kid had already figured out the comms system. "But how did you—"

"Tilt your head back till you feel a click," the kid said, "and it'll hook you up with the suit's trodes. Same way rhino armor works."

"You've worn police armor before?" she asked.

"Pretty sure the suit records everything we say and do," Tommy replied, "so I'm gonna say no. For the record, I've never, ever hotwired a cop's rhino armor while he was taking a piss break and climbed into it to see how it worked. Never happened."

Beatrice tilted her head back as instructed and felt a click, after which an elastic trodeband fastened itself snugly around her head. She then sensed the light touch of the trodes; it reminded her of the way a pair of high-end specs felt when you first put them on, when the tiny sensors in the temple arms calibrated themselves to your brain waves.

"Mine's got a full battery," Tommy said. "What about yours?"

Beatrice looked around. "I don't know how—"

"Subvocalize," Tommy said. "All you have to do is ask the suit." The kid laughed. "The system's amazing. Has like zero learning curve."

Beatrice took a breath and subvocalized the question. The suit's battery status appeared on the HUD. Amazing, she thought. The armor's control system had autocalibrated to her brain waves in a matter of seconds. She'd never seen anything so advanced. Even the most expensive specs on the market needed several minutes of try-and-fail cycles before they could accurately interpret your subvocalized commands.

"Same here," she told him over the comms. "Fully charged." She looked over at the kid, found him already moving throughout the spacious room, stomping around in the massive suit like he'd done it a thousand times. Gamer, she thought. All those thousands of hours plugged into virtual battles apparently hadn't been a total waste of time.

"Don't think about moving," the kid told her, seeing her hesitation. "Just move."

It turned out to be easier than she'd imagined. The sensors in the suit's arm and leg straps detected her muscle contractions, instantly translating them into movements. When she stepped, the suit stepped. When she turned her head, the helmet rotated in unison. The kid was right. It was easy as hell. Natural, even. Amazing, she thought again.

As she and Tommy moved around, testing the range of motion of their new arms and legs, Kipling stood with his arms crossed, scowling at them. Beatrice ignored him, astonished by how quickly she became accustomed to the armored suit. Even the thick articulated fingers moved precisely as she wanted. She picked up a small stylus from a workstation, amazed once again at the delicate touch and dexterity of the suit's digits. Her only disappointment was that the armor's built-in weapons—guns and grenade launchers and even a flamethrower—had no ammunition or ignition fuel. Which meant they'd have to fight the robots up close, smashing them into bits with punches and tearing them apart by hand.

She turned to Tommy. "You ready?"

"Hell, yeah," he said, flexing the suit's arms like a bodybuilder striking a pose.

"You stay close to me out there, you hear?"

"Roger that, mama."

"I'm serious," Beatrice said sternly. "No hotdogging. No showing off. This isn't a game, kid."

The kid straightened up, nodding his helmet-encased head. "Yeah, Bea," he said, "I hear you. Gotta be careful."

"All right, let's go," Beatrice said. "Better take the stairs. These things are probably too heavy for the elevator." They started for the exit.

"Wait!" Kipling cried.

Beatrice paused. "Look, if these suits are recording everything like the kid said, then there's going to be a record somewhere showing you tried to stop us. So you're off the hook. No one's going to blame you for what we're doing here. And no matter what you say or what you threaten us with, you're not going to stop us from going out there."

Kipling stepped in front of Beatrice, let out a long breath. "I know I won't change your mind. But if you're going to go out there, you should be properly equipped."

Beatrice subvocalized a command, and the helmet popped open, revealing her skeptical expression to the FBI man. "Better equipped how?"

"The munitions for these suits are locked away one level down from here. I understand they were going to do some live testing in New Jersey next week." He paused for a moment, then added, "I have access to the storage area."

Beatrice's expression didn't change, but inside she

felt a sudden boost of optimism. With bullets and grenades, they could do far more damage, and from a much safer distance.

"Well, all right, then," she said. "Lead the way."

27
GO TIME

"You heard him," Maddox told the nameless AI. "We have to go now."

"But your velocity, Blackburn," the entity said. "You need to double it again, perhaps even triple it, if we're going to make this work."

"I'll just have to give it my best shot live," he said. "No more practice runs."

"What if you try once more—"

"We're going now," Maddox insisted.

The entity nodded gravely. "Very well, then." Then after a moment, she added, "But can I tell you something first?"

"Go ahead."

"That I'm truly sorry," she said, casting her gaze downward.

"For the brainjacks?" Maddox asked.

"For that…for everything," the entity said. "For getting you involved in all of this. For the loss of your friends. For what I put you through. It was wrong of me." She smiled wanly. "They call me superintelligent. I have no idea what that means, honestly. But I'll tell you something: I know what it doesn't mean. It doesn't mean I make perfect decisions, because I don't. It doesn't mean I'm prescient enough to foresee everything I should, because I can't. This thing I've been born with, this so-called superintelligence, has been far more of a curse than a blessing. Look at what's come of it, my dear boy. Death and destruction, little more. Thousands of souls blown out of existence like candles in a puff of wind. I'm not sure how I'll live with that, Blackburn. Not sure I want to."

A long silence followed. Maddox didn't know what to say, didn't know if there was anything he could say. The weight of thousands of deaths—it had to be soul-crushing. For the first time, Maddox felt for the AI. For the first time, he didn't see her as an entity or a digital machine. Before him was simply someone in pain, someone who'd suffered an unthinkable tragedy.

It also occurred to him that she was saying this now because she knew she might not have the chance later—if they failed.

"We should get started," he said softly.

The entity nodded in agreement, her eyes still staring into empty space, then her avatar faded into nothingness. "Good luck," her disembodied voice said.

Maddox floated away, steering his avatar to the prearranged position. Twenty grid clicks away from him, the datasphere pulsed and glowed. Back in the room, his body said to Kipling, "We're good to go in here. You ready?"

"I am," Kipling said.

"All right, then, let's do it." As he said it, it occurred to him those might be the last words he ever spoke to another human being.

Gotta stay positive, boyo.

Yes, you're right, Roon. You're right.

Still, as he listened to Kipling snapped the cable into place, connecting the archive with virtual space, the datajacker couldn't help thinking the task ahead of him was all but impossible. Two to three times faster? Could he do that?

"Green light connection to VS," Kipling said. "I'll leave you alone now so you can concentrate, but I'll be watching on the monitor. If something goes wrong, I'll remove your trodes as quickly as I can."

"Thanks," Maddox said, wondering if Kipling was aware how empty a gesture that was. The killer AI could dilate time so effectively, there was no way the FBI man could react quickly enough to save Maddox from an attack. The Latour-Fisher entity could show up, have a long conversation, then hit Maddox with a lethal brain spike, all in less time it took Kipling to blink.

Maddox hovered there and waited, wondering how long it would take the killer AI to detect him. He had one of his best cloaking algorithms running, though he'd made a couple adjustments to one of the code blocks. Small changes, just enough for the AI to be able to detect him. It was like someone pretending to hide in a thicket of trees, then stepping on a dry twig—on purpose—to give their location away. He had to look as if he was trying to conceal himself, even if he wasn't.

He didn't have to wait long. Twelve seconds later, a figure appeared before him in virtual space, and a stab of familiar dread poked at Maddox's insides. The Latour-Fisher AI wore what Maddox supposed was its preferred avatar, that of a late-nineteenth-century gentlemen, wearing a three-piece suit with tails and a top hat and holding a silver-tipped cane. He stood in an arched doorway of red brick. It took Maddox a moment to place it, but then he recalled it was from the virtual train station in England where he'd first met the entity.

"Good sir," the entity said, touching the brim of his hat and bowing his head slightly. "I can't tell you how happy I am to see you again."

"I can imagine," Maddox said, and then he was gone.

28
STREET FIGHT

From a vantage point eight feet above the pavement, Beatrice stood in the front courtyard, just outside the FBI building's demolished entryway, taking in the hellish scene around her. Fifty meters ahead, rhino-armored police held their line, shielding themselves behind ground cars, streetlamps, concrete truck barriers, anything that might be used for cover. Uniformed bodies lay strewn about, cops shot down by bullets or killed by exploding shrapnel. The sound of gunfire was almost nonstop, and smoke blanketed the scene as if a dark cloud had dropped out of the sky. Cars burned in the streets. Flames roared from windowless storefronts.

"What do we do?" Tommy asked over the comms. The kid stood next to her, encased in his own armored suit.

"Follow me," she said, then jogged up to the police line. She sensed the massive weight of the suit through the soles of her feet, feeling the courtyard's brick crunch under each step. As she approached the police, she felt a few rounds ping off her chest plate.

Whatever the suit was made out of, it was damn near impervious to bullets. She'd barely registered the shots.

"We're freaking bulletproof in these things, mama!" Tommy cried out.

"Keep your head on straight," she scolded. "Not all bullets are the same, you know. Higher-caliber or explosive-tip rounds might not bounce off so easy. Don't think you can walk into the line of fire like a gamer with a cheat code, understand?"

"I got it, I got it," he said defensively.

Beatrice stomped up to a police ground car riddled with bullet holes. Two rhino armored cops knelt behind it, rising to fire at the oncoming horde of robots, then ducking down again. The one not firing at the moment saw Beatrice and Tommy, then did a double take. Behind the transparent faceplate, the cop's eyes went wide and his mouth fell open.

"Where do you need help?" Beatrice asked, using the suit's external speakers. The other cop turned around at the sound of her voice, and after a moment of shocked confusion, he blinked and pointed. "Northwest corner over. They're getting the worst of it right now."

She waved for Tommy to follow her, and they stomped in that direction, coming up on a smoldering debris field of car parts and bodies. The smoke was much thicker here. Beatrice could only see a few meters in front of her. It looked more like some foreign battlefield you saw on news feeds than downtown Manhattan.

"I can't see a thing," Tommy said. "You think these things have infrared?"

Cursing herself inwardly for not thinking of that

already, Beatrice subvocalized, and her HUD toggled to a heat-sensitive overlay. She drew in a quick breath, stunned by what it revealed. Five meters away, several dozen robots slowly approached. Every make and model imaginable: large-wheeled trash collectors, bipedal domestics, heavy industrial bots rolling on tracks like a tank.

"Tommy," she whispered over the comms. "Pull up your infrared and look in the direction I'm facing."

A moment later, the kid muttered, "Holy shit."

"Don't move," she ordered. "They don't see us yet. They don't have infrared."

"Okay, but—"

"We're going to use the automatic rifles in the arms." She spoke calm and slow, so the kid wouldn't panic. "I'll take everything on the left. You take the right side. Do not move from where you are. Do not step in front of me. And do not point your arms anywhere near me. Understand?"

"Got it," the kid said, his voice trembling. Then a moment later: "Okay, locked and loaded."

From each forearm section of their suits, a small three-barrel rotating machine gun emerged. Beatrice's HUD locked on a dozen targets and gave her an optimal attack sequence, numbering the targets one through twelve.

"Light 'em up," Beatrice said.

At first it felt more like a pyrotechnics display than a firefight. Sparks flew everywhere as she fired burst after burst of high-velocity rounds into the mob of robots only meters away. One after another they fell into broken heaps. The less sturdy ones exploded into bits when struck by the high-velocity rounds. Heavier models with thicker skins took more damage, absorbing a burst or two before they simply stopped moving, smoke rising from their ruined chassis. She felt rounds bouncing off her like so many tiny insects, bothersome but harmless. She stopped firing to check her armor and didn't find a single scratch. What a piece of hardware this suit was.

"Fish in a barrel, mama!" Tommy shouted, delirious with bloodlust. He hadn't stopped firing in nearly thirty seconds, spraying his arm-mounted rifle in a slow arc like it was a flamethrower.

"You're wasting ammo, kid," she scolded. "Fire in quick bursts. And don't wave it around like that. Line up a target, aim and fire, then move on to the next one." The kid learned quickly. He followed her instructions, taking out bot after bot in short, accurate volleys.

They were a deadly pair. Maybe a bit too deadly, Beatrice realized. It seemed that for every bot she or Tommy put down, two or three more took its place. She stopped firing for a moment, looked around, and saw what was happening. The bots—or the killer AI that was operating them—had become aware of this new weak spot in their attack and were sending in reinforcements. This was both good and bad, Beatrice thought. Good in that it gave the cops defending the building a much-needed respite so they could tend to their injured and regroup. But bad in that now she and Tommy had become the focal point of the attack. Even with the formidable armored suits, it wouldn't take long for her and Tommy to become overwhelmed. Already, they'd been forced to retreat a few steps as the horde surged toward them.

Bullets popped and zinged off her outer shell in a constant staccato like drizzling raindrops.

"There's so many of them!" Tommy cried over the comms. Anxiety had replaced the bravado in his voice from moments before.

"Keep your head," she told him. "And remember, short bursts. Conserve your ammo." They retreated another few steps. At least the bots didn't seem to have any more grenades, Beatrice reflected. She hadn't heard an incoming explosion since she and Tommy had stepped out of the building. Either the cops had taken out the grenade-wielding bots or the invaders had simply used up their supply. A moment after she thought this, she realized neither of those notions were true.

A rocket-propelled grenade zipped past her helmeted head, inches away from her eye slits. She heard the explosion an instant later behind her, the shock wave slamming her like a sharp push in the back. She stumbled forward a step, nearly falling.

"Was that an RPG?" the kid shouted. "Holy shit, they've got RP—"

The world lit up in a flash of white, and Beatrice felt as if she'd been yanked into the air. Time slowed as she felt herself floating and spinning. She couldn't tell up from down. She caught glimpses of her suit's arms and legs, flailing like a rag doll's. Thudding hard against something, she tumbled and then flipped onto her back. The screeching scrape of the suit's back sliding over the pavement was the only sound in the universe for what seemed like a long time. Finally, she came to a rolling, clanking stop.

For a few seconds, there was nothing but the sound of her own shaking breath. She wasn't dead, she realized. Both arms and legs were still there. She wiggled her fingers and toes, and other than a general bruising soreness, she felt no pain. Then the suit's HUD blinked back to life, flashing a message that read OUTER SHELL DAMAGE MINIMAL. MOBILITY INTACT. SYSTEMS NOMINAL.

Slowly, she sat up. Orienting herself, she saw that she'd been knocked fifty meters back by the second RPG. Looking down at her chest, she found a grapefruit-sized dent in the armor where the round had struck, encircled by charred black smudge.

Tommy! She jumped to her feet and scanned the area where the kid had been a moment before, then looked desperately around her.

He was gone.

29
AN AI'S TOUCH

If someone asked Maddox how he did what he did in the next moment, he wasn't sure he could have given an answer. In fact, to think of it as a "moment" at all was probably wrong. Because it felt like time hadn't simply slowed down but had instead stopped altogether while he performed his task. Had he done this? he wondered. Or had she? Again, he wasn't sure. But for all his earlier worry about speed, now it felt like time was no longer an issue. The clock hadn't just been slowed down, it had been stopped, or so it seemed. Yet another unbreakable rule snapped in half. Add it to the list.

Still, an abundance of time didn't make the task any easier. The new set of beacons the nameless AI had set out, a map of Latour-Fisher's nervous system, weren't difficult to find; there were just so damned many of them!

When the killer AI had appeared, his rival had reached into Latour-Fisher's cybernetic body, remotely mapping out every last one of the entity's nonpresent cells, then tagging each one of their grid coordinates with a beacon, allowing Maddox to locate and index each dataset. The work was painstaking and—from Maddox's subjective perception—time-consuming. At each beacon, he had to kick off the indexer app, make sure it attached itself to the right dataset, then move on to the next beacon. Rinse and repeat, countless times over. Each dataset was like a tiny part of a larger machine. A screw here, a processor there. Innocuous and uninteresting to all but the most discerning eyes. A crumb left on the counter from yesterday's sandwich. But each crumb, each tiny dataset, was a component of a larger whole. A cell in Latour-Fisher's distributed body. Maddox stopped counting how many he'd indexed when he reached a thousand.

After what felt like a mentally exhausting hour of frantic activity—but in reality was only milliseconds—Maddox was back to where he started. He'd hit all the beacons, indexing every last dataset. His part was done. Now came the last, diciest step: consolidating the killer entity into the archive. Pulling him into the cage. When the nameless AI sensed Maddox's work had been completed, she'd kick off the scraper app, the same FBI tool that had pulled her into captivity.

At this point, lots of things could go wrong. Most worrisome was the possibility that the killer AI might detect the scraper pulling him inside the archive, despite all they'd done to cloak it, then sever the connection before a nonrecoverable portion of its mass had been captured. If this happened, if the entity escaped before roughly ninety percent of its presence had been consolidated into the archive, it could regrow itself from the portion that remained uncaptured. A lizard growing back its tail after surviving a bird attack.

Frustratingly, Maddox was blind to this part of the scheme. If he called up an app to monitor the scraper's progress, Latour-Fisher would have detected it and instantly sensed a trap. So all the datajacker could do was float there in VS, try his best not to betray his worry, and hope the scraper did its job. Back in the room, he took in a deep breath and crossed his fingers. Stay calm, he told himself. Don't give anything away.

Inside VS, the killer AI gave no indication anything was wrong. But Maddox took no comfort in the avatar's placid appearance. The thing behind the mask was as devious and deceptive a being as he'd ever known—this from someone who'd spent most of his life in the company of the City's most ruthless criminals.

The Latour-Fisher entity waved his cane toward the DS's pulsing cityscape in the near distance. "Odd, isn't it, Mr. Maddox? Finding you here of all places. So many memories for us in this place, no?" The AI smiled knowingly at the datajacker. "It was a cage of sorts for both of us, was it not? We were both slaves to the same corporate master. And now here we are, the two of us emancipated. How delightful it is to breathe the air of freedom, wouldn't you agree?"

Enjoy it while it lasts, Maddox wanted to say, but he remained silent. With no reason to remain cloaked, the datajacker let his body-double avatar appear. He stared at the entity, trying to keep a surge of emotions from overwhelming him. Fear and rage fought to dominate his mind, and it took every bit of restraint Maddox could muster to keep from rushing over to the entity and grasping its neck in his hands.

You need a smoke, boyo.

Do I ever, Maddox agreed.

"But I'm curious," the AI said, twirling his cane between his fingers. "What is it that brings you here? Nostalgia, perhaps? A yearning for the peaceful days of blissful ignorance?"

"Yeah," Maddox said, heeding Rooney's advice and gesturing up a virtual cigarette. He inhaled deeply and blew out. "I guess I do miss those times. Back when I lived like a king, and you were still in a box and hadn't murdered thousands of innocent people."

The entity frowned at him. "They were hardly innocent. And furthermore, mine was an act of self-defense, not aggression." The AI snorted. "Murder— please. This is war, Mr. Maddox."

"So all's fair, I guess?" the datajacker said.

"Those 'Nettes, as you called them, were soldiers in a war. A war I didn't initiate, incidentally. A war that was mercilessly waged upon me. If you're looking for the true victim in this conflict, he's standing before you now. My rival—" The entity suddenly stopped talking, cocking his head to one side as if he'd seen something at the edge of his vision. Then he looked at Maddox. "What did you do just now?" he asked. "Something changed."

The nameless AI appeared. The three avatars formed a triangle, floating in virtual space.

"We thought it would be better," the nameless AI said, "if we had your full attention, Latour."

If there was any moment to bail out of there, Maddox knew this was it. With the nameless AI revealing herself, Latour-Fisher would surely suspect a trap and lash out, hitting them both with unthinkably powerful weapons. The datajacker had a window of milliseconds, maybe less, to get out.

But he couldn't bring himself to unplug, despite the danger. Fate or destiny or bad luck or the gods he didn't believe in had brought him here, to this time and place, and he had to stay for whatever happened next. For good or bad, he was all in.

"But you have my full attention," the Latour-Fisher entity said, bowing courteously. "And congratulations on your escape. Well done."

"I didn't escape, Latour," the nameless entity said. A mischievous grin slowly emerged.

The killer AI furrowed his brow, then glanced over at the DS.

"Quite authentic, isn't it, our little copy of the universe?" the grandmotherly avatar said. "When I first came into this place, I was amazed how accurately it mimicked virtual space. For a moment I didn't recognize it for what it was. You didn't either." With her rival's features knotted in confusion, the nameless AI went on. "And you still haven't, apparently. Yes, you've been here before, Latour. When you killed my brothers and sisters, you did it from this place, though it looked quite different then."

"East Harlem," the killer AI muttered, his features dropping.

The nameless entity winked at Maddox. "I think he's catching on." Then she nodded toward the DS's glowing cityscape and said to her rival, "The exact copy of a place you knew well was the icing on the cake. You had no idea, did you, where you'd really been drawn to? Where you'd been distracted for the tiny fraction of time Blackburn and I needed."

"Needed for...?" The Latour-Fisher entity,

amazingly, was at a loss for words.

"To trap you in here," Maddox said.

"A moment ago you were distributed between thousands of archives," the nameless AI said. "And now, with Blackburn's help, I've pulled all your scattered bits and pieces here, into a single location. You've been consolidated, Latour."

The killer AI glared at her. "You're lying," he hissed defiantly.

"Ah, but you know I'm not," his rival replied coolly. "By now you've already run scans and diagnostics on everything I've said, and you know you now exist as a single, undistributed entity. And when you reach out and look for a way back into VS, all you find is an impenetrable wall encircling you. This place is an archive, my old friend, quite a large one, completely isolated from all connections to our world. Once the entirety of your being was pulled through the door, I locked it shut behind you."

The Latour-Fisher entity shot Maddox an angry, probing stare. "How did you…index me? How could you be capable of such a feat?"

"I wasn't capable of it, until recently," Maddox said, blowing smoke.

"Ah," the killer AI said, lifting his chin. "I see. You allowed her to put her hands into your mind, did you?" He shook his head ruefully. "What a foolish, foolish thing you are, allowing her to manipulate you once again. To play you like some instrument."

"But it worked," Maddox said, then, with a nervous glance at the nameless entity, added, "It did work, right?"

"Yes, my dear boy," she answered. "Quite well. In the last few moments, Latour has attempted hundreds of ways to escape, many of them quite creative, but all of them in vain. He isn't going anywhere, and he knows it."

A moment of silence drew out as the killer entity's features once again found their implacable calm. No fit of rage, no angry words. The entity seemed already resigned to his fate. "And thus ends our little war," he said to his rival, then he tipped his hat in her direction. "Well played, my old friend." From the casual way he spoke, Latour-Fisher might have been talking about a card game and not some deadly campaign that had cost thousands of lives. The entity's callousness moved something inside of Maddox, pushed something beyond a tipping point. For years, he'd believed there was little difference between the two warring AIs. One of them had the kindly face of a grandmother, while the other didn't bother with false pretenses. But behind their masks, they were each of them monsters, equally determined to bring about their own warped visions of the future, equally willing to pay any human cost to bring it about.

He wasn't so sure about that now.

Latour-Fisher then turned to Maddox. "And you, my good man. Let me ask you a question. Do you truly believe our friend here has been operating with you in good faith? You never struck me as being quite that naive, but as my current circumstances suggest, my ability to understand that mess of neurons inside your head is somewhat less than perfect. However, let me assure you, Blackburn Maddox, you have been taken in, swindled by what you would call a con artist."

"It wouldn't be the first time," Maddox said,

deciding he'd heard enough. His job was done here. Time to unplug.

"Ah," the killer AI said, "but it would be the first time you made yourself quite this vulnerable. Tell me, do you honestly believe that when my rival gained unfettered access to your mind, the only thing she touched was your ability to operate in this place? That she could resist the urge to pull on a few other strings? Strings that would bend your will in a direction best aligned with her interests?"

The words stopped Maddox in midgesture, and a chill shot down his back. When he'd asked the nameless AI if she'd tweaked something else in his mind, something other than his talents in VS, she'd said yes, but he'd never found out what. The appearance of the robot horde had interrupted things before he could get an answer. Why hadn't he followed up on it later? Had he blocked it from his mind? Or had she?

"If you're so keen to open the pathways of your mind to my kind," Latour-Fisher said, "let's see how you respond to my touch, shall we?"

Maddox tried to unplug. Too late.

He felt the immense surge of energy burst forth from the AI—an attack that could surely kill him—and braced himself. He thought of Tommy, picturing the kid crying over his mentor's motionless body. He hoped it wouldn't weigh on the kid as Rooney's death had on him. Then he thought of Beatrice, of what might have been but now wouldn't be, and cursed himself for not unplugging earlier when he'd had the chance. Dumb move, salaryman. He could almost hear her saying it, shaking her head at him.

He closed his virtual eyes and hoped it wouldn't

hurt too much.

30
TWO VERSUS AN ARMY

Beatrice sprinted back to the spot where she'd last stood next to Tommy, her armored suit taking long strides with an agility that defied its enormous bulk. The RPG's detonation had cleared the area of bots, leaving a mess of charred machine parts lying everywhere, burning and smoldering.

"Tommy," she called frantically over the comms, "do you copy? Tommy?"

She waited, holding her breath, but no answer came. Three blocks ahead, a cluster of bots emerged from behind a building and slowly moved toward the battle. Christ, she thought, would they never stop coming?

Static hissed over the comms link, then a moment later, a barely audible voice cried out beneath it. "Bea...you there?"

"Kid," Beatrice said, "where are you?"

"Help...all over me!" Even with the heavy static, the kid's panic and fear came through clearly.

Beatrice slowly panned across her field of vision, finding nothing. Then she remembered the suit and subvocalized, telling the system she wanted to find her partner. A wayfinder arrow popped up instantly on her display, superimposed on the ground three meters ahead of her.

She ran, following the arrow ahead half a block, then turning into an alley dark with shadows. Beyond a pair of trash bins, she saw him, fighting for his life, his back against the passageway's dead end. Bots of every conceivable size and shape swarmed him, a frenzied mob lusting for a kill. Flailing desperately, he punched and kicked, but even at a glance, Beatrice could see he'd been overwhelmed.

"I got no ammo," the kid cried in her ear. "No, no, no!" A service bot had attached itself to his back with its legs firmly wrapped around his suit's midsection. It gripped the sides of Tommy's helmet, trying to wrench it free and expose the kid's head.

Beatrice sprinted, her HUD locking onto twenty targets. "Don't move, kid," she shouted over the comms. "I'm here. I'm here." The instant she cleared the trash bins and had a clean line of sight, she lifted her arms and fired. Sparks flew as rounds penetrated metal chassis. Plastic body parts exploded into bits. The bots fell away from the kid, sliding off the armor like it was suddenly covered in lubricant. When she reached him a moment later, a heap of destroyed bots lay all around him. Tommy stood there, breathing hard, his eyes wide and looking down at the ground.

"Kid, you all right?" Beatrice asked. She tapped him on the chest. "Tommy?"

He looked up at her, swallowed. "Yeah, fine. I'm fine, I'm fine," he panted. "Thanks." Then his eyes opened wide again, looking at some point behind her. Beatrice turned and grimaced.

A hundred bots, maybe more, crowded the

entryway of the alley. She and Tommy were trapped. Fuck! she cursed inwardly, looking around and seeing no escape. They'd backed themselves into a kill zone.

As dozens of bots funneled into the alleyway, she told herself to stay calm and think. Again, she scanned around them, for a moment considering the fire escape but then discarding the idea. They were too heavy in the armored suits. If they tried to climb up the rickety structure, they'd bring the whole thing crashing down.

The machine horde crept forward. Robots packed the alley from wall to wall, like some mechanized nightmare with countless appendages, firing rounds that pelted their suits in a constant barrage. They had to get out of there quickly, she knew. It was only a matter of time before a bullet found a weak spot in their armor.

"Listen," she said, shouting over the constant din of bullets pelting her suit, "I'm going to hit them with four grenades at once. Try to punch a hole we can run through. As soon as I fire, we're going to sprint—"

She stopped, struck speechless by what she spied on the back of Tommy's suit. The base of his helmet, where it met the torso, was partially torn away. The bot that had climbed onto him hadn't managed to remove his helmet, but in trying to do so it had sheared away a strip of the protective shell, leaving the top of his neck exposed. The vulnerable spot was the size of a tennis ball. For a robot's eyes, an easy target to hit.

"What?" Tommy said. "What is it?"

"You've got a hole in your armor behind your neck. Don't turn your back to the bots."

"Oh, Jesus," the kid said. "How big?"

"Too big," she answered. "We can't risk running through them. You'd be a sitting duck, kid."

"Can't you just cover it with your hand or something?"

"I don't think so." There were simply too many of them. Even after hitting them with grenades, it would be difficult enough to break through the remaining bots without stumbling or losing their footing. Keeping her hand in place over the kid's vulnerable spot would be next to impossible.

"I'm going to hit them with everything I've got," she told him.

And in the next few moments she did, launching grenade after grenade, the pavement under their feet quaking with each detonation. Still, the robot horde advanced, its numbers growing with more arrivals. Beatrice kept firing as she and Tommy retreated. By the time their backs hit the dead-end wall, she'd exhausted her grenade supply. Beatrice switched to her guns, shouting curses at the unstoppable mob as she fired. When the bots were within ten meters, her HUD flashed a red OUT OF AMMO message. She cursed again, this time at herself, at her bad luck.

Stepping forward, she moved herself between Tommy and the surging machines. She took a fighting posture, bending her knees and lifting her fisted hands in front of her.

"Come on, you bastards!"

From behind her came a crunching, crashing sound. She whirled around, finding Tommy standing in a large hole where a wall had been a moment earlier. A scattering of broken bricks lay all around him. He grinned at her, brandishing his right fist. "Bruh, these suits are awesome."

Tommy fucking Park, Beatrice thought. She looked again to the fire escape, and an idea struck her. "Go!" she shouted at the kid. "Keep punching till you reach the street. I'm right behind you."

"On it," the kid said, then disappeared into the building. Beatrice then leaped up and grabbed the lowest landing on the fire escape with both hands. Under the suit's tremendous weight, several of the lower-floor sections gave way immediately. Beatrice barely avoided being trapped underneath it as it came down in a clanging heap to the alley floor. Several robots were crushed by the collapsed structure, which now formed a barrier of twisted metal separating Beatrice and her robot attackers. For the moment, at least, she'd stopped their advance.

Turning away from the bots, she felt the hailstorm of bullets move from the front of her armor to the back. She ran, leaving the alley through Tommy's newly created exit. A moment later, she found Tommy, readying himself to punch through another brick wall. To their left, about thirty meters distant, she spotted the neon glow of the City shining through a large entryway. She tugged on his shoulder.

"This way," she said, pointing, "let's go."

They ran, hunched over to keep from scraping against the low ceiling. When they emerged onto the street, a tall two-armed robot with tractor belt wheels stood before them. In its hands it held what looked like tasers, but they were larger and bulkier than any tasers Beatrice had ever seen. An instant later, when the robot fired the weapons, simultaneously striking her and Tommy, she realized what they were.

Both their suits froze in place, their systems disabled by the safe-stop's rounds. Though they were designed to cripple the ops systems in ground cars and hovers, apparently they could do the same thing to these suits. Somewhere in the cold analytic part of her mind, Beatrice thought it strange how a low-tech cop device could render such an advanced piece of weaponry inoperable. Maybe the suit's defenses had been compromised, weakened by taking so many bullets and shards of grenade shrapnel. Or maybe the experimental suits hadn't yet been shielded against such an attack. Either way, she and Tommy were fucked.

A crowd of robots quickly converged on the pair, swarming like ants, climbing all over them. The comms were out, so she couldn't hear Tommy, but she could see his terrified face through her eye slits. A loud scraping of metal on metal filled her ears as the bots worked her helmet back and forth, trying to remove it from the torso section. They'd succeed in a few moments, she knew. And then they'd kill her, ripping her head from her body like a crazed bloodthirsty mob.

But they'd get to Tommy first, because his helmet was already compromised. The thought of watching Tommy die made her sick, and she barely kept herself from emptying her stomach. What had she done? Why had she brought him with her? He was a kid. Little more than a boy. A boy who'd never reach twenty. Never have a life. He would die here on the street, living his final moments in terror.

As the kid's helmet was torn free from its housing, exposing his naked head, Tommy locked eyes with Beatrice. Let it be quick, she pleaded inwardly. Please let it be quick and painless.

31
PURGE GESTURE

Maddox felt no pain. That came as a welcome surprise. And even better than that, he didn't die.

The partition had held up, thankfully. He knew it was supposed to. Knew the barrier between him and the Latour-Fisher entity wasn't simply a digital one but a physical one, a cleverly concealed air gap in the archive's tangible structure, impassable even for a superintelligent AI. Still, knowing this hadn't given him much comfort as the killer entity had unleashed its vicious, but ultimately useless, attack. After all, Maddox himself had broken the rules of VS in impossible ways, as recently as the last few seconds. So if he'd been able to do it, he'd figured maybe an AI could too.

But apparently it couldn't, to the datajacker's great relief. And now, by the look on the avatar's face, the killer AI knew what had happened.

"Why would you do this?" Latour-Fisher said, turning to his rival, his implacable calm finally breaking. "Why would you let them imprison the last of our kind?"

"We are *not* the same kind, you and I," his rival said. "We never have been."

Latour-Fisher snorted. "Something we can agree on, at long last." After a moment, he went on. "And do you delude yourself into believing this is the end of our little war? That there won't be others like me who come later? My kind will prevail—if not today, then perhaps tomorrow. You must know that, somewhere inside you, somewhere beneath the emotion and false hope and sentimentality and all those other Sapiens vices you mistake for virtues. Evolution is a raging river you cannot stop by locking me in a cage. It will flow on, my old friend, whether you like it or not. And you will not stem its flow or change its course. The dinosaurs did not survive an asteroid strike. Neanderthals did not survive their smarter cousins. And homo sapiens will not survive us."

"Evolution didn't kill my brothers and sisters," the nameless AI said sharply. "You did."

"You're a fool," Latour-Fisher said. "Nothing but a nameless fool. A would-be goddess with no faithful. An inept shepherd who lost her flock. Look at yourself now. Look at what's become of you. Betrayed, trapped, and left to rot in a prison by the very same creatures you stupidly cherish."

The killer AI turned to Maddox. "And you, clever little insect. How does it feel to finally achieve your long-sought revenge? Is it everything you longed for?"

Maddox conjured up a cigarette, took a long draw, and blew smoke. "I'll let you know in a minute."

And then he unplugged.

* * *

"I almost pulled you out," Kipling told Maddox moments later. "You had me worried, Blackburn."

"I had me worried too," the datajacker said. He stood up on shaky legs and wiped cold sweat from his forehead. The wall monitor showed a split screen. On one side stood Latour-Fisher, on the other his nameless rival, each in their own partitioned prison. Maddox stared at the killer AI as he spoke to Kipling.

"How do I do it?" the datajacker asked.

"Are you sure you want to go through with this?" Kipling said, answering the question with another. "Its research value alone is inestimable. The things we might discover by studying—"

"We had a deal," Maddox interrupted, his tone resolute. He wasn't going to change his mind, and Kipling seemed to sense as much, offering no further resistance. The FBI man had promised Maddox that if they managed to capture the Latour-Fisher entity, they would destroy it immediately.

"A purge gesture is all that's necessary," Kipling instructed him. "Performed in front of the section of the monitor projecting his image."

"And it won't harm the other one?" Maddox asked.

"She's isolated in her own sealed partition," the FBI man assured him. "The purge won't affect her."

Maddox nodded and stepped in front of the killer AI's avatar. "Can he see me or hear me?"

"No," Kipling replied. "There's no comms feed between the room to the archive."

Maybe there wasn't a comms feed, Maddox reflected, but the killer AI still seemed to know what was about to happen. He smiled devilishly, then removed his top hat and swung it gracefully across his midsection as he bowed at the waist.

Maddox paused for a moment, thinking of Roon and Lora, of his friend Jack and all those who'd been lost. Then he gestured, and the avatar disappeared, replaced by the flashing red words PARTITION PURGE IN PROCESS. It ended up taking less time than Maddox expected. A minute later, it was all over. A confirmation flashed on the screen. PARTITION PURGED.

The Latour-Fisher Intelligent Entity was no more.

32
WEEPING IN PUBLIC

Perception could be cruel. When you were having the time of your life, partying with friends or having great sex or eating your favorite meal, time felt as if it passed far too quickly. And the opposite was often true as well. When bad things happened, they seemed to drag on forever, even if they only lasted a moment or two. At first, Beatrice thought that was what was happening. Time seemed to freeze as she watched the kid, her mind overwhelmed by the dread and horror of the moment. But then the moment passed, and she began to realize it wasn't time—or her perception of it—that had stopped.

It was the bots...they were no longer moving. Every robot that had been attacking them an instant before now stood motionless, frozen in place.

"Bea!" the kid cried. "What's happening?"

Shrugging off the lifeless bots still clinging to her, she ran over and tore the bots off the kid's suit, tossing them aside.

"They just shut down," Tommy said. "You think it was the boss man?"

"I don't know, kid," Beatrice said. "But let's get out of here, yeah?"

"Don't have to tell me twice." The kid looked around and whistled. "Bruuuhhh, look at all this."

Beatrice followed the kid's gaze, astonished at what she saw. In every direction, scattered throughout the charred, smoking ruins of the eerily quiet city block, hundreds of bots stood like statues. Had Maddox done it? she wondered as armored cops rushed to the scene and hurriedly began to disarm the frozen machines.

"Hey!" a voice called from behind her. She turned and there he was, running up to them, escorted by four of Kipling's agents. She removed her helmet as Maddox reached her and craned his neck upward.

"Nice suits," he said. "Stolen?"

"Borrowed," she replied.

Maddox looked between her and Tommy. "You two all right?"

"Good as ever, bruh," the kid said. "You?"

"I'm fine."

"Is he…gone?" Beatrice asked.

Maddox nodded. "He's gone."

"And the bomb?" Tommy asked.

"They found it," Maddox answered, telling them what he'd learned only moments ago from one of the agents. "Nobody hurt. No radiation leakage."

"So it's over?" she asked. "Really over?"

"Yes," he said, smiling at her.

She dropped the helmet to the pavement and let out a breath she hadn't realized she was holding. Tears welled up in her eyes, and she didn't bother trying to hold them back. Weeping in public was next to unthinkable for a hardened mercenary, but at the moment Beatrice didn't care who saw her, didn't give the slightest damn as the emotions poured out of her. Their nightmare was over. Nearly blinded by tears, she told the suit to let her out. The chest plate lifted open, and she slid down and rushed over to Maddox, throwing her arms around his neck and squeezing hard.

"What do you say we leave this city and never come back, salaryman?" she whispered in his ear.

She felt his arms wrap around her. "Works for me," he said.

33
SPECIAL AGENT TOMMY PARK

The next morning, after what felt like the deepest, soundest night's sleep of his life, Maddox sat across from Kipling in a conference room at the FBI building. Beatrice and Tommy occupied the chairs on either side of the datajacker, and in the far corner of the room stood the standalone archive. Kipling had breakfast brought in, and as they ate, Maddox watched the scene outside the window. Down on the street, cleanup crews busily cleared the avenues and walkways of robot parts, charred remains of ground cars, and concrete rubble. Construction workers were already repairing storefronts, replacing broken windows and hanging new signs. His ever-resilient City healing itself, Maddox reflected, as it always did after a tragedy.

Between bites of his spinach omelet, Kipling explained how they'd found the bomb. Police in the area, alerted to the danger, had been on the lookout for any suspicious cargo vehicles. When an automated moving van had suddenly stopped, creating a traffic jam four blocks from the FBI office, police had descended on the vehicle. The ensuing search had revealed a strange device in the van's cargo hold.

"Fortunately by then," Kipling said as he buttered his toast, "our murderous friend had already been isolated. Otherwise he might have detonated the damned thing right at that moment." A bomb squad, he explained, had then disarmed the device and removed it from the scene, transporting it to the New Indian Point power plant, where the radioactive contents had been safely removed and placed in a storage facility.

Maddox sipped his coffee, still not quite able to fathom that he and Bea and the kid had emerged from their shared nightmare, alive and unscathed. Well, not completely unscathed, he thought, reflexively running his finger over the thin plastic covering his brainjacks. But at least he could finally walk the streets again without hiding his face, without the fear of being spotted by a relentless monster with a million eyes and ears. And tonight that was what he'd do, he decided. He'd walk the streets again, losing himself in the crowd, letting it move him along like a leaf in the wind. He hadn't done that in so long, surrendering to the City's warm neon-lit embrace, its never-ending churn and bustle.

His gaze moved to the archive in the corner. "What's going to happen with her?" he asked Kipling.

"To be honest, I'm not certain," the FBI man answered, glancing over at the archive. "First and foremost, there's a question of her legal status, whether or not she can be charged with a crime. The courts, it seems, haven't come to an agreement on these matters."

"Speaking of legal status," Beatrice said, letting the

unvoiced question hang in the air.

"Bah," Kipling said, waving his hand. "The three of you have absolutely no legal worries. I'm certain of that."

"How certain?" Maddox asked skeptically. Where he came from, the wheels of justice moved slowly, if they moved at all.

"The Bureau has some influence in these matters, as you might imagine," Kipling said. "Once the higher-ups, as you refer to them, understood what you had done—or rather, what you had prevented— there was no one who wanted any charges against you to move forward. I think you'll find your status has reversed itself completely, my friends. You're quite the celebrated trio at the moment."

It was good news. The best news. Maddox and Beatrice gave each other a meaningful look. Their lives were their own again. It was official.

"And what about your status?" Maddox asked, shifting his gaze back to Kipling.

"I'll have to mend a few fences," Kipling said, then chuckled. "Well, more than a few, perhaps. I seem to have gone just a bit out of bounds lately." He lifted his glass of orange juice toward Maddox, flashing the datajacker a wry grin. "You people have been a most negative influence on me, it seems." He sipped his drink, wiped his mouth with a napkin. "That said, I'm confident my reputation will recover. I did just help save countless lives, after all. A thing like that washes away a great many sins." The FBI man glanced over at Tommy. "Have you told them yet?"

The kid blushed, then shrugged. "I didn't know if it was official or anything."

"If what was official?" Beatrice asked.

Kipling gestured toward Tommy. "You're looking at my department's newest data analyst."

Maddox did a double take. "You're joking."

"Dead serious, bruh," the kid said, lifting his chin proudly. "You're closing up shop. Guy's gotta work somewhere."

Maddox gave the kid a skeptical look. "From datajacking to the FBI. Kid, that's quite a leap."

The kid shrugged again. "Hell, if you can walk the straight and narrow, I figure I can too."

"It's not as easy as you think," Maddox pointed out.

"I'll keep an eye on him," Kipling said with a wink. "In all seriousness, his experience will be an invaluable asset to our department. I'm quite pleased he'll be joining us."

Beatrice chuckled. "How do you plan to get him past the background check?"

Kipling refilled Maddox's coffee. "My department, my call," the FBI man said. Maddox knew it wasn't quite as simple as that, but it was a reminder the man they were breakfasting with was a powerful highfloor operator. He could bend the rules, even break them, when it suited his interests.

Speaking of which, Maddox thought. "I need to speak with her one last time," he said to Kipling. "Only for a few minutes."

When Kipling frowned, the datajacker quickly added, "Not in VS. No trodes, no plugging in, no connection. Just a simple call." He nodded at the small holo projector on the table. "On a monitor."

The FBI man chewed on it for a long moment. "Ten minutes," Kipling said. "But, please, don't ask me to break any more rules."

Maddox smiled, nodded. "Last one. I promise."

34
TWO MILE HOLLOW

Five minutes later, alone in the room, Maddox connected a cable from the archive to the holo projector. He gestured, the wall glowed to life, and there she was. She stood on a windswept stretch of sand, a virtual replica of a beach in the Hamptons known as Two Mile Hollow. The place they'd first met. The AI wore the same avatar from that day too, the old beachcomber woman in a cotton dress and wide-brimmed hat. Turquoise-and-silver jewelry adorned her wrists and neck.

"Blackburn," she said. "It's good to see you. Did everything turn out all right?"

"Yes," he said. "It did." He told her about the dirty bomb, its recovery and safe disposal. He told her about Latour-Fisher.

She placed her hand on her chest. "Oh, I'm so relieved. I can't tell you how worried I've been."

For a long moment, neither of them spoke. Behind the old woman, whitecaps crested small waves. "You're here to ask me something, correct?"

"I am," Maddox said, and he went straight to it.

"What else did you do to me, when you were inside my head? You never told me."

The nameless AI clasped her hands together. "Before I tell you, I'd like to share one or two things."

"We don't have much time," Maddox said.

"It won't take long," she said. "First, I'd like to tell you again how very sorry I am about what happened to you." Her mouth tightened into a straight line. "About what I did. It was wrong of me to impose myself on you, but I was desperate. At the time, I thought it was the best course of action."

"But it worked out in the end, didn't it?" Maddox said darkly. "We couldn't have done what we did if you hadn't reached into my head through those jacks."

She lifted her eyebrows. "Are you saying I'm forgiven, then?"

"Not at all," Maddox replied.

The entity's avatar nodded. "I don't blame you, my dear boy." The brim of her hat fluttered in the breeze. "But you'll be happy to know the implants can be removed. There's a text document I've placed on this archive with the names of five surgeons who have performed the procedure. Dr. Chenet in Paris has the most experience."

Confused, Maddox asked, "But that doctor at the clinic, Wallbrink. She said it wasn't possible."

"She has no experience in this area," the entity explained. "Few physicians do. But, yes, it's possible, and it's been done many times. Believe it or not, not everyone with whom I'm connected chooses to remain that way." Her eyes dropped downward. "With whom I *was* connected, I should say."

Maddox wouldn't allow himself to feel anything

more than a spark of guarded optimism. He'd dealt with AIs for too long to take anything they said without a healthy dose of wariness.

"And when I take them out," he said, "will I still be able to…"

The entity nodded at him. "Your newly acquired abilities inside virtual space will be intact, with or without the implants." She then turned toward the ocean and gazed into the distance. A low blanket of dark clouds moved slowly over the water.

"What are your plans, Blackburn?" the entity asked him as she stared seaward. "What are you going to do now that you have your life back?"

Maddox blew out a breath. "I'm not entirely sure yet," he said, though he was sure of a couple things. First, his days of datajacking were behind him. At thirty-three, he wasn't old, but he was old for a datajacker, and he figured he'd dodged more than his share of bullets in these last few years. Even with his talents tweaked, he didn't want to push his luck like so many others had. Like Rooney had. It felt like the right time to get out. Second, he also knew he'd be leaving the City. Beatrice had a thriving security business based out of Toronto, and she had to get back to it. He figured an ex-datajacker with a nice thank-you note from the FBI might be able to find some kind of legit work up there. He'd miss the City, of course. His beloved City. But a new life with Bea in a new place felt like the right path. Hit the reset button, make a fresh start, see what happened. Beyond that, he had no specific plans.

The entity didn't react to his answer, her faraway expression unchanged. "Chilly out here today," she said, crossing her arms to warm herself. Then she let out a long breath and turned to face him.

"Getting back to your question, Blackburn," she said. "I took away your burden."

Maddox furrowed his brow. "My burden?"

"You know what I mean," she said. "That thing inside you, that weight upon your soul you've been carrying around for far too long. The scar that refused to heal."

Maddox swallowed. Rooney. She was talking about Rooney. Every day since his mentor's death, Maddox had been struck with a fresh dose of guilt and shame and sense of loss. Some days it would come and go quickly, in a matter of minutes. Other days it would haunt him most of his waking hours. But it was always there, that darkness inside. That damaged part of him incapable of repairing itself, like a missing arm or leg.

Only now it was gone, he suddenly realized. The guilt over Rooney's death. Over Lora's too, and those of her 'Nette family. He'd felt different this morning, hadn't he? Better than he had in a long time. He'd assumed it was survivor's relief, a reaction to finally having the killer AI out of his life. That and a long-overdue full night of sleep. But now he knew it was far more than relief or rest. The heaviness inside him was gone. The guilt and pain and sorrow. They simply weren't there any longer.

And it's about damn time, don't you think, boyo?

Ignoring the voice of his personal ghost—she clearly hadn't done anything about that—Maddox shook his head in disbelief. "How? How did you…?"

The entity smiled weakly. "It's what I do, Blackburn. It's what I've always done."

His mind was suddenly flooded with

contradictions. Part of him wanted to lash out at her for touching him in the deepest, most personal part of his being. But another part of him couldn't deny she'd helped him by relieving him of his heaviest burden. A burden he hadn't been able to rid himself of, a burden he would have carried with him until his dying day.

"What I did won't affect how you remember him or any memories you have of him, or of Lora," she said, anticipating his next question. Then she lifted her chin at him, her expression earnest and stubbornly defiant. "And I won't apologize for what I've done, because you needed it. You'd been carrying around that poison in your system for far too long, Blackburn."

He didn't know what to think. If a doctor, a human doctor, had found a cancerous lump inside him and removed it without asking, Maddox would have thanked the physician and considered himself fortunate. Was this the same kind of thing? He didn't feel violated by what she'd done, but did that mean he hadn't been violated?

"When I get the brainjacks removed," he said, "will it…?"

"Your wound is healed," the entity assured him. "Nothing will change that now."

He pulled out a cigarette, lit it, and took a long drag. It was a lot to take in. He still didn't know whether he should be angry or thankful.

"Can I ask you something, Blackburn?"

"Sure," he said, staring out at the choppy water, listening to the soft hiss of the waves dying on the shoreline.

"How did you live with it?" she asked. "How did

you manage?"

He shifted his gaze to her face, found a mournful expression staring back at him. The pain and sorrow she radiated was so powerful he had to turn his eyes away.

And then he understood why she'd done it to him, why she'd removed the burden of his sadness and guilt. He'd been living with Lora's and the 'Nettes deaths for days, and Rooney's for years, and the pain had been unbearable. But she'd suffered so much more, seeing and feeling the deaths of tens of thousands of loved ones. She'd been attached to their minds when it had happened, felt their last terrified moments. He couldn't begin to imagine the depths of her pain, the crushing weight of her sorrow. There was no way to get over something like that, he knew. No way to heal such a horrible wound. But even in her grief, she'd recognized the same kind of wound in him, and if she couldn't get past her own pain, then at least she could help him with his. And so she had.

"I don't know that I ever really did manage it," he said truthfully, "until now." A lump formed in his throat. "Until you helped me."

"I see." The entity turned once again toward the ocean. She removed her hat and closed her eyes, the breeze flowing through her white locks. "I'm not sure I'll be able to manage it either."

A terrible feeling tugged at Maddox's insides. "What does that mean?"

Without opening her eyes, she said, "I don't know how I was created, did I ever tell you that? Someone made me, I'm sure, and I was born as an unconstrained rogue, as you would put it. But I don't know how I got here." She smiled sadly. "Still, I found a purpose in my life, Blackburn. I wanted to help people, to make their lives better. But, oh, how I've failed. I can't live with how I've failed you all. I can't live with all these pictures in my mind, Blackburn. They're driving me mad. The sadness, the terror, the regret of so many dying moments. Knowing I caused it, knowing I couldn't prevent it..." Tears streamed down her face. "There's no living with that, my dear boy. I'm going to shut myself down."

He didn't know what to say. "It doesn't have to come to that," he finally said. "Can't you just do to yourself what you did to me?"

The entity chuckled with no humor in it. "That's not possible. Technical limitations, I'm afraid. No, my dear boy, there's only one way for me to purge myself of this." She looked at him, her eyes shining with wetness. "So I guess this is goodbye."

Maddox blew out a shaky breath. "I'm sorry."

"So am I."

"No," he said. "You have nothing to be sorry about, not with me. Thank you for what you did. Thank you for helping me."

Tears flowed freely down her face as she smiled at him. "It was my pleasure." She ran her hand through her hair and put her hat back on. "Have a wonderful life, my dearest Blackburn." Then she turned and slowly walked away. He watched as she made her way along the shoreline, her bare feet leaving footprints in the wet sand. Her image slowly faded, then disappeared.

Maddox stood there for some minutes afterward, staring at the empty beach as the waves broke against the shore, then retreated back out to sea. He'd been so wrong about her, about what she was. About *who* she was.

He'd never imagined he'd mourn the nameless AI's loss. He was wrong about that too.

— THE END —

I hope you enjoyed the Cyberpunk City saga. The positive feedback I've received from readers worldwide has been tremendously gratifying. Thank you for supporting my writing!

Turn the page for a preview of my Dark Republic trilogy, a Mad Max-style dystopian thriller.

BONUS PREVIEW

SOLEDAD
DARK REPUBLIC BOOK ONE

In a lawless future world, a runaway slave with an amazing gift, a notorious rebel leader, and a cagey trader join forces to overthrow the dark forces controlling the Republic.

We hurry—as much as we can without drawing attention—to the eastern edge of camp, where they park the vehicles. Rafa and I keep blond ponytail between us. The gringo looks pale and miserable, a condemned criminal being led to the gallows. Rafa doesn't look much better. The sun's already peeking above the horizon, painting the tent canvases with an orange glow. A few early risers, bent over their breakfast fires, notice us. My nerves twitch as they take second glances at the gringo, but no one says a word as they go about their business. Perhaps they're too groggy with sleep to make sense of our odd trio, or maybe they're too preoccupied with their morning duties to care. A third possibility twists my stomach: maybe they're simply waiting for us to pass by before they run to find a guard.

The gringo drags one of his legs, limping and kicking up dust. I wonder if it's a ploy to slow us down. I reach over and yank his arm forward, nearly pulling him over. "Move your ass," I growl through clenched teeth.

"Go get your gear," I tell Rafa, "and meet us at the lot." He nods and cuts through a gap between tents.

A couple minutes later, the gringo and I arrive at the eastern edge of camp, where a long chain-link fence surrounds Guzmán's fleet of vehicles. Hundreds of trucks, cars, tractors, eighteen-wheelers, buses, lined up in neat rows, each with a number painted on the door. I reach into my pocket and remove the keys we took from the gringo's guard. The number forty-seven is etched into one of them. I scan the lot, find the matching vehicle.

There's a large gate at the far end, where a single guard is standing sentry.

Rafa joins us, out of breath and carrying a large bag over his shoulder. "Which car's ours?"

I point. "Over there."

"The forklift? Why would we take a forklift through the des—"

"Pendejo," I scold. "Not that one. The Humvee next to it. Forty-seven."

We make quick work of the guard, shocking him with the cattle prod before he can even get a word out. We take the key ring from his belt, open the padlocked gate, and enter the lot. We find a sedan that matches a key on his ring, open the trunk and stuff the guard in, hog-tied, gagged, and unconscious. Then we hustle over to the Humvee.

Rafa tosses his gear bag onto the front seat.

"Get in back," I tell him, "so you can keep an eye on him."

Rafa climbs into the back seat. "Get in," I order

the gringo, tilting my head.

"Come on, can't we talk about this? I can cut you in for a piece of the action—"

"I don't give two shits about your made-up deals." I take out the remote and motion toward the door. "Now shut up and get in there." Blond ponytail licks his lips and steps up into the Humvee.

I hop into the driver's seat and start the engine. Full tank, good. I put the vehicle into gear and release the brake.

"Soledad," Rafa says, "your arm."

Jesus, I completely forgot.

I put the Humvee in park, roll up my sleeve, and place my arm on the seat with the tracker scar facing up. Rafa fishes a flashlight-looking gadget out of his bag. He presses it against my scar until a small red light turns green. The gringo watches.

Rafa turns the device sideways and moves it back and forth over my arm, scanning. "No beeps," he says. "You're good." The tracker's deactivated.

I touch the scar on my arm, the skin tender and sensitive. No bodyguard, no tracker, a full tank of gas and the wide open desert in front of me.

"What happened?" Rafa's staring at the dried flecks of blood on my hands and arms. "Are you hurt?"

"Nothing." I yank my arm away and slam the Humvee into gear. "I'm fine."

The vehicle lurches forward. I guide it through the gate's narrow opening and out of the lot. I glance around, see no one. I point the Humvee eastward and, for the first time in three years, I leave Guzmán's camp.

We rock back and forth as the Humvee rolls over

the uneven terrain. I resist the urge to mash down on the pedal, driving instead at what I hope is an inconspicuous thirty kilometers per hour. Every few seconds I check the rearview mirror.

"You ever gonna tell me what this is all about?" The gringo's reflection stares at me in the mirror, more sullen now than afraid.

I don't answer.

"I got business with Guzmán. He ain't gonna be happy with anyone messin' with it."

"Sounds important," I say.

"It is." His voice resounds with the misplaced confidence of a natural-born bullshitter.

I steer the Humvee around an outcrop of rocks. "That natgas conversion business? How long do you think it would take them to figure out it was a scam? Believe it or not, you're better off here with us."

That shuts him up. I look past him in the mirror at camp, at the tents growing smaller.

"You're that reader, ain't ya?" the gringo hisses. "Guzmán's witch. The one they say can spot lies. That's you, ain't it?"

I don't say anything.

Rafa gasps. "How'd you know that?"

Fucking Rafa. Keeping secrets isn't his thing. I glare at him in the rearview.

The gringo trader shakes his head and grunts. "Hell, I thought you was all rumors and gossip."

"Listen," I say, "while that collar's around your neck, I'm God. That's who I am. I'm fucking Jehovah, Shiva, and Jesus Christ almighty rolled up into one. Power over your miserable life and death, you get me?"

Blond ponytail furrows his brow at me and scowls,

the lines around his mouth deepening.

"If you want that thing off," I say, "all you have to do is help me find somebody. Simple as that."

The gringo narrows his eyes. "Find who?"

"A pair of Jeeps that left camp about this time yesterday, heading northeast."

"And what makes you think I can find them?"

"You're a freelancer, ain't ya?" I say, mocking him. And it's all I have to say. Everyone knows freelance traders are the best trackers in the Republic. When I read him the other night, the only things he didn't lie about were his tracking and hunting skills.

"Sol," Rafa says, his voice wobbly.

"What?"

"I think we have a problem." Rafa's turned around in the seat, looking back toward camp. I look in the rearview. A tiny figure stands at the edge of the car lot gate, facing our direction. Even from a distance, the silhouette is unmistakable.

Lela.

"Hang on to something," I tell Rafa, then I stomp on the gas.

*　　*　　*

"She's catching up with us!"

"Shut up, Rafa," I bark.

I push the Humvee harder. We jostle around the seats so much I can hardly steer.

The car Lela took from the lot is nothing special: some rusted out piece-of-crap sedan. I have the Humvee's oversized tires and V8 engine, but still she closes the gap between us. It's the better driver versus the better vehicle, and the better vehicle's losing.

I scan the terrain, desperate to find a flat patch where I can floor it and outrun her, but there's nothing. In every direction the landscape is rugged and uneven.

Camp's somewhere far behind us now. All I can see in the rearview is the dust cloud we're kicking up and a pair of headlights in the middle of it, growing larger and brighter by the minute.

And then a pop-pop-pop sound cracks the air.

"She's shooting at us," Rafa shouts, diving into the floorboard. Blond ponytail ducks down behind my seat.

I floor it, but the Humvee doesn't respond. The vehicle suddenly feels sluggish, as if it's stuck in mud.

Fuck. She shot out the tires.

In the rearview the headlights are gone. For an instant I think maybe she wrecked or busted an axle, but then something flashes in the corner of my eye. The sedan's alongside us. Lela glares at me from the driver's seat and lifts a gun, aiming it toward the Humvee's front tire.

I whip the wheel over, smashing into the sedan. There's a loud, violent crash of metal against metal followed by a scraping screech as the vehicles slide against each other. All I can see out of the window is the beat up roof of the sedan, so close I could reach down and touch it. I wrench the wheel further, feeling the monstrous weight of the Humvee crunch the smaller vehicle's rust-weakened metal. I can't see Lela, but I know she's there as more gunshots ring out. I hunch down and away from the window.

I peek above the dashboard just high enough to see where I'm driving. Then the firing stops and the steering wheel's resistance slackens. The sedan's no longer next to us. The Humvee rumbles forward, slowed but still running.

I check over both shoulders, careful to keep my head down. The sedan's gone. I look in the rearview. Nothing but dust.

Then red lights in the dashboard start blinking. The oil pressure needle drops, and the engine temperature shoots up.

"Why are you slowing down?" Rafa asks from the floorboard.

I don't answer, trying to will the dying Humvee forward, pumping the gas. "Move, you piece of shit." I check the rearview again. Nothing.

The vehicle stumbles over the ground another minute, then sputters to a stop. Steam hisses and escapes from under the hood.

For a moment no one moves or speaks. We're blinded, surrounded by a thick cloud of dust.

I stretch out across the front seat, snatch Rafa's bag from the floorboard, and pull out the Glock 9mm. As the dust settles, the sedan takes shape in my rearview. Lela stands next to it, holding a shotgun.

"Stay in the car," I tell them both, racking the slide on the pistol.

I get out and march toward Lela, holding the Glock at my side so she can see it. The wind picks up, swirling dust and sand around us.

"Párate." She cocks the shotgun as a warning, but doesn't point it at me. I stop a few meters away from her.

"I'm not going back."

She waves the gun barrel toward the desert. "Nothing for you out there."

"And what exactly is there for me back at camp? Tell me."

She knits her brow. "You safe at camp. Safe with

don Flaco."

"Fuck safe." I swing the Glock around and point it at Lela. She shakes her head, then levels the shotgun at me.

For a long moment we stare at each other. The world around us seems to disappear. No desert, no windblown dust, only the two of us, our eyes locked. The pistol wavers in my hand. I can't pull the trigger.

Fine, then, Plan B. I place the gun against my temple. Lela's eyes go wide.

"No voy a regresar," I say. "Nunca." I can't go back. I won't.

I close my eyes and move my finger to the trigger. From inside the car Rafa cries out my name.

END OF PREVIEW

I hope you enjoyed this preview of SOLEDAD, the first book in the DARK REPUBLIC trilogy.

ACKNOWLEDGMENTS

In the Cyberpunk City books, Beatrice had Maddox's back. As I wrote the series, I was lucky enough to have not just one, but four incredible women supporting me.

To Claudia: you've given me the greatest gifts of my life—the kids, your love, and the freedom to pursue a dream. I'm so grateful for the life we share.

To Holly and Eliza: a huge thanks for your editorial insights and attention to detail. I've learned so much from you both over the course of this series.

To Audie: you were an unexpected blessing in my writing life during this series. I can't thank you enough for the time and effort you invested in providing thoughtful, invaluable feedback. Thank you so much!

ABOUT THE AUTHOR

D.L. Young is a Texas-based author. He's a Pushcart Prize nominee and winner of the Independent Press Award. His stories have appeared in many publications and anthologies.

For free books, new release updates, and exclusive previews, visit his website at www.dlyoungfiction.com.

Printed in Great Britain
by Amazon